FELIX
& THE MESSIAH

The Adventures of Felix, a Secret Agent Angel

by B.G. Clyde & Felix, SAA

FREILING
PUBLISHING

Published by Freiling Publishing, a division of Freiling Agency, LLC.

P.O. Box 1264,
Warrenton, VA 20188

www.FreilingPublishing.com

ISBN 978-1-950948-34-5

Printed in the United States of America

Table of Contents

Jerusalem........................1

Ethiopia........................13

Judean Hills....................17

Nazareth........................21

Road to Hebron..................29

Judean Village..................33

Nazareth........................41

A Carpenter's House.............49

Nazareth........................59

Bethlehem.......................67

Susa............................77

Jerusalem.......................85

Bethlehem.......................95

Egypt...........................103

Nazareth........................117

Jerusalem.......................123

Nazareth 133

Jordan River 139

Judean Wilderness 153

Cana 159

Sea of Galilee 165

Capernaum 173

Galilee 179

Hillside in Galilee 187

Northern Israel 195

Jerusalem 199

Bethany 203

The Road to Bethel 209

Bethany 213

Jericho 217

Jerusalem 225

Jerusalem, the Upper Room 233

Jerusalem, Trials 237

Jerusalem, Calvary 245

In and Around Jerusalem 253

Outside Jerusalem. 261

Galilee 271

Road to Jerusalem 277

Heaven 281

Map of
Israel
in the
Time of
Jesus

Capernaum

Cana

Sea of
Galilee

Nazareth

Jordan River

Jericho

Jerusalem

Bethlehem

Bethany

Dead Sea

Hebron

← Egypt

Ethiopia

Jerusalem

This was the best day in five hundred years, but it did not start well. Philos and I were heading to Meditation Point when a force whooshed past me. I was flipped upside down and round and round. When I finally stopped, I yelled for Philos to wait.

"Keep up, slow poke!" Philos laughed. "Am I moving too fast for you?"

"See that silver glow?" I replied. "Is that Gabriel?"

"I think so. Where is God's chief messenger going in such a rush?"

"Earth," I said. "Secret Agent Angels [SAAs] go to Earth all the time, but a major angel hasn't been there in centuries."

Philos turned toward the Crystal Sea.

"Where are you going?" I shouted.

"Obeying the new command," Philos replied.

"What new command?"

"You must have felt the jolt of an All Angel Command to come to the Crystal Sea," Philos said. "Check your receptors. You must have gotten it."

I spun around and could feel the air rushing around me. My receptors were working fine. I would have felt the jolt of an All Angel Command. "My receptors are working fine," I answered.

"I'll meet you at Meditation Point when I'm finished," Philos said as he zipped toward the Crystal Sea where God has his throne. "Maybe you weren't summoned because you're on probation!" he yelled as he disappeared from sight.

It wasn't fair. I was curious; I admit it. I was on probation because I didn't get my work done in heaven. Instead, I checked on the people I helped on Earth. I was assigned only easy missions, such as getting produce to market or cleaning fish. Now,

I was not even allowed to go to the Crystal Sea to worship God.

I stood there wondering. Where was Gabriel going? What was his message? I wanted to follow him. I almost jumped into the cosmos, but no. My curiosity was going to get me into more trouble. The commander said I must regain his trust; I must obey all orders.

I turned and looked toward the Crystal Sea. Angels were headed there from everywhere. Why wasn't I ordered to go there? I wanted to follow Philos. I wouldn't get into too much trouble for following him. I started toward the Crystal Sea, but it felt wrong. Mediation Point was where I was ordered to go, so there I headed.

Suddenly, I felt a tingle and saw a hologram of young boy lost outside Jerusalem. I was off to Earth, to Jerusalem. Maybe Gabriel would be there. With a shout of Eloooree (Angelic for "Glory to God"), I took a running leap into the cosmos and went streaking toward Earth.

As I entered Earth's atmosphere, I tucked into a ball to slow my descent. It was just before sunrise when I landed outside Jerusalem in an olive grove. I was a twelve-year-old boy. How was I going to find my boy, my mission?

I stepped into the main path and landed with a THUD on the ground. Someone was screaming, "Let me go! Let me go!" and was beating on me.

"Ouch! Stop hitting me!" I yelled. "I'm not holding you."

The hitting stopped, and the screaming was replaced with sniffling. A boy about six years old was lying on top of me. His nose was running and tears streamed from his eyes.

"That's better," I said as I stood up and brushed the dirt from my robe. "My name is Felix; what's yours?"

"I'm Joab," he stammered as I helped him stand.

"Why are you crying?" I asked.

"My mother hurt her foot, bad," he replied.

"You were crying because your mother got hurt?"

"No, the mean men are trying to kidnap me," Joab said.

"Let's start at the beginning. What happened?"

"My father and brothers went to morning prayers at the temple; they said I was too young to go," Joab explained. "I was mad and didn't fold up my blanket like Mama said. She was carrying a heavy pot of water and tripped on my blanket. She hurt her foot really bad; she can't even stand on it."

I nodded my head and motioned for Joab to continue.

"The other women came to help. I was trying to help. My sister said I was in the way. She ordered me to leave and not come back until the sun was high in the sky."

"Then what happened?" I asked.

"I wanted my father. I was walking toward the temple when I heard some men talking. I just wanted to know what they were talking about. When they saw me, one of them yelled, 'Look, a boy! Grab him. We could sell him.'"

"Wow. No wonder you were running," I replied. "Curiosity can get you into trouble, I know."

"I thought you were one of them," Joab said.

"Hey, boy, come here. I'm not going to hurt you. Come here, boy!" someone shouted.

"The men, run!" Joab yelled.

"Too late. Let's hide in the bushes over there. Be quiet," I ordered. We crept to the bushes near the olive trees and squatted down ready to run if we had to.

Soon, three men appeared. The leader was a young man, but his face and arms were scarred, and he carried knife in his hand. He called, "boy!" The other two men argued that "boy" wasn't worth enough to bother with. Joab fell backward and yelled out.

"Did you hear that? I bet it's that boy," the leader said. He started walking toward us. I grabbed Joab's hand, ready to jump up and run.

"Listen! Horses; Romans. They're looking for us. Let's go, Ferox!" the other men yelled.

"I'll be back for you, boy!" Ferox yelled as he ran away.

Soon, Romans on horseback clattered down the path toward Jerusalem.

"I think we're safe," I said. "We need to get you back to your family. Are you camping here in the olive groves?

"Yes," Joab answered.

"Good. Which way to your camp?" I asked.

"I don't know. It was dark, and I ran a long way. I'm lost. I don't know where my mother is. I don't know where my father is," Joab said as he began to cry.

You might wonder why I didn't use a superpower to discover where Joab's family was camping. SAAs don't have that type of superpower. We can be anyone we need to be. We can speak any language we need to speak. We can have any talent or skill we need. We don't have superpowers such as super hearing or the ability to fly. We can fly only between heaven and Earth.

I realized that Joab did know something that would help me find his family.

"That's not quite right, Joab," I said as I knelt down. "You do know where your father is. He's at the temple. Let's go to the temple."

I noticed that the white and gold walls of the temple were washed with the pinks and yellows of the sunrise. I knew we must hurry; morning prayers would start soon.

"Can you run fast? We need to get to the temple before sunrise," I told Joab.

"Faster than those men."

"Eloooree! Let's go!" I yelled as we dashed through a gate.

"What did you yell?" he asked.

"Eloooree!" I yelled again. "It's a word I use when I begin an adventure."

"Eloooree!" he yelled as we zigged and zagged through the narrow streets.

When we heard the braying of sheep and goats, I knew we were near the temple. The shouts and clanging of the moneychangers told me we had entered the temple grounds. We rushed to the center of the temple complex.

"Abba, Daddy!" Joab yelled as he dragged me toward a man.

"Joab, what are you doing here?"

"I'm so sorry, Abba. I didn't mean for Mama to fall. Please forgive me, Daddy."

"Joab, what are you talking about?"

Between sniffles, Joab told the whole story. "Felix brought me to the temple to find you," Joab said as he pointed to me.

I nodded to Joab's father.

"Thank you, my son, thank you. How can I repay you? My name is Jabak."

"I'm glad we found you, sir," I replied. "Have we missed morning prayers?"

"They're just beginning," Jabak responded. "Zechariah has been chosen to burn the incense. He's a good man."

"You know him?" I asked as I watched an old man prepare the incense.

"A little; he lives in the Judean hills near Hebron," Jabak said. "He and his wife, Elizabeth, are good people. We could use more people like them, but they have no children."

I nodded and watched as Zechariah entered the Holy Place and stepped toward the golden altar of incense. With my angel eyes, I saw Gabriel's light shining next to the altar. No one else could see Gabriel's glow. *What message was Gabriel bringing to Zechariah?* I wondered.

Soon, the sweet and spicy scent of the burning incense filled the air. This was the holy moment when everyone in the temple was silent and offered prayers to God. I prayed for Zechariah and wondered what Gabriel was saying to him.

I felt a tug on my robe. Joab whispered to me, "I prayed for my mama."

I smiled and nodded.

We waited and waited for Zechariah to return, but he did not appear.

Jabak said, "I wonder if Zechariah has fallen or gotten sick. He's so old."

Suddenly, Zechariah stepped out of the Holy Place with his arms raised above his head and a smile spread across his face.

The priests spoke to Zechariah, but he said nothing. He just smiled. Flapping his arms, he tried to show that an angel had spoken to him, but no one understood—no one but me, that is. I knew Zechariah had seen Gabriel.

"He's seen an angel!" I shouted.

"I hope you're right, but Zechariah may have breathed in too much incense," Jabak said. Several others laughed at me, and some called me a fool. Zechariah nodded his head yes.

"Eloooree!" Joab yelled. I laughed, but then I thought, *You're right, Joab. Israel is starting a great adventure.* I just wasn't sure what it was.

I said goodbye to Jabak, Joab, and his brothers. As they walked away, I heard Jabak tell Joab that he would be his mother's personal servant until her foot was completely healed.

I went into an alley in Jerusalem and shouted, "Eloooree!" as I did a triple somersault in the air and sped back to heaven.

I hurried to tell Philos about my mission. Philos, Spero, Gaudo, and several other SAAs were sitting at Meditation Point. I explained that Gabriel had spoken to Zechariah, but I didn't know what Gabriel had said.

"I think we know," Spero answered. "All the angels were told Earth will be blessed with the coming of the Messiah."

"The Anointed One!"

"The King of Kings!"

"The Lord of Lords!"

"The Prince of Peace!"

"The Son!"

"The Savior!"

Each SAA shouted one of the many names given to the one promised to help people know God better.

"He will be called Jesus. SAAs will introduce people to Jesus and encourage them to listen to him," Gaudo explained.

"Did Gabriel tell Zechariah that Elizabeth would give birth to the Savior?" I asked.

"No," Philos said. "Elizabeth will give birth to the one who comes before the Savior. Remember Malachi said that God would send a messenger to prepare the way for the Savior."

"Eloooree!" I yelled.

"Eloooree!" shouted Spero.

"Eloooree!" chimed in Philos.

"Eloooree!" cried Gaudo.

Suddenly, all the SAAs were swooping, spinning, and praising God.

Ethiopia

I was entering my last missions in the celestial database. Joab was easy, but Barabbas was a problem. Barabbas was a young man heading down the wrong path. I tried to redirect him, but I failed. He stole some pears from my fruit stall. When I questioned him about the pears, he denied having them. This wasn't the first time he had stolen or lied. In his life plan, I saw a decision point coming up soon. I requested an SAA mission to guide him to the right decision. A thousand SAA requests aren't as powerful as one human prayer. I also requested that an SAA would go to his parents and encourage them to pray for Barabbas.

As I closed Barabbas' record, the commander sat down next to me. "I'm glad to see that you are getting your entries into the database. You're improving, Felix," the commander said. "I'm rewarding your hard work by sending you on a special mission to Ethiopia."

"Ethiopia!" I yelled. "Wow, that's great but scary. What will I do there? When do I go?"

"You will sell these star charts and Jewish prophecies in the marketplace," the commander answered. "You leave now. I look forward to reading your report in the database as soon as you get back."

I flipped and twirled around, yelled Eloooree! and leapt into the cosmos.

I couldn't believe I was going to Africa. Just seeing the sights would be enough to satisfy my curiosity. Watch out, Africa, here I come.

I landed on the coast of Ethiopia and set up my stall in a local market. What a fabulous place. Traders came from Egypt, Arabia, India, and Persia. The aroma of exotic spices filled the air, and the roars of wild animals echoed through the market. I loved to feel the smooth silks and sleek furs that hung in stalls. Gold and diamonds glittered at the back of some stalls.

My days were exciting, but the nights were even better. Merchants from many places sat around a campfire eating a salty fish stew and discussing the religions of the world. I tried to make them understand about the one true God. Some were interested and some weren't. When the moon was high in the sky, I rolled up in my cloak and watched the stars until I fell asleep. Ethiopia was great.

Too quickly, all my charts and scrolls were gone. There was still so much to see and do. I asked to stay longer, but I was told no. The commander was beginning to trust me, so this was no time to disobey. I gave my stall to the ivory merchant next to me, walked over the hill, yelled "Eloooree!" and zipped back to heaven.

As soon as I arrived in heaven, I sat down to begin my report on Ethiopia. I glanced toward Earth and saw an old man running through the Judean hills. I switched my eyes to telescopic (SAAs can do that when we are in heaven) and looked closer. It was Zechariah. I forgot all about my report on Ethiopia.

Judean Hills

Travelers stared as an old man with his robe gathered in his hands ran by them. When he stopped to catch his breath, a traveler said, "Slow down, old man; you're going to hurt yourself!"

Zechariah pointed down the road and started to run. He ran for three days, ate little, and slept less.

Elizabeth was sitting outside her house grinding cumin. She heard feet pounding on the road and looked up. Zachariah was bent over, trying to catch his breath. Grabbing a dipper and a jug of water, she ran to him.

"Oh, Zechariah, I'm so glad you are home," Elizabeth said. "Tell me everything that happened in Jerusalem. What jobs did you do at the temple? Who did you see there?"

Gulping the water, Zechariah smiled at Elizabeth and spun her around.

She laughed, "What's the matter with you?"

Zechariah just smiled.

Elizabeth frowned and felt her husband's wrinkled forehead. "Say something. What's the matter, Zachariah? Are you sick?"

Zechariah shook his head no, no, no. He jumped around, trying to pantomime an angel. Elizabeth stared at him. He knelt down and wrote in the dirt: "We're going to have a baby, a boy."

"No, no, no, it's not possible," Elizabeth whispered.

Zechariah nodded yes, yes, yes.

I felt a hand on my shoulder. "Felix, I looked for your report on Ethiopia and couldn't find it," the commander said.

"I had started it when I saw Zechariah," I stammered. "I'm sorry. I'll do it right now."

"Yes, you will," the commander said. "Oh, Felix, what am I going to do with you? This is how you got in trouble in the first place. You were to go to

Ethiopia, write a report, and wait for your next mission. Instead, you watched Elizabeth and Zechariah. They weren't even your mission; Joab was. Ethiopia was."

"I know, but important events are happening on Earth; Elizabeth is going to have a baby. I just wanted to watch."

"I'm extending your probation. Don't expect any exciting missions for a while. You will also be the proofreader and fact checker on the database. Get to work."

"Yes, sir."

The commander left, and I started writing my report. When it was finished, I wandered to the Reflection Grotto. "Why do we even have proofreaders and fact checkers?" I grumbled. "It's boring; no mistakes have ever been found, not even a misspelling."

A voice said, "We have fact checkers and proofreaders because it is boring and you need to obey orders. Get to work, Felix."

"Yes, sir," I said as clapped my hands to bring up the database.

Nazareth

After three weeks of harvesting barley on Earth, I was zipping back to heaven as fast as I could. There's no pain in heaven, but there's lots of pain on Earth. Sunburned back, sore shoulders, bruised legs, and blistered fingers in my case. Suddenly, a silver force flashed by me.

"Yikes!" I yelled as I spun upside down and round and round.

Where was Gabriel going this time? I had to watch. Why was he going to Earth again so soon? Did it have something to do with the Savior going to Earth? Gabriel was heading toward Galilee in northern Israel.

I wanted to watch, but I needed to write my report on harvesting barley. Before opening the database, I switched on my telescopic vision for one quick peek. Gabriel landed in a meadow west of Nazareth.

"Nazareth?" I mused, "Philos and Spero, both SAAs, had been sent to Nazareth several months ago." I reviewed what I knew about their mission.

Philos and Spero lived in Nazareth as husband and wife. Philos was an olive oil merchant and Speria was his wife. They lived next door to Anne and her daughter Mary. Speria and Anne frequently worked in their gardens together.

Anne and her husband Joachim were from Cana. They moved to Nazareth where they owned an olive grove. Joachim died when Mary was a little girl; his brothers ran the business and cared for Anne and her family.

When Mary was a teenager, her uncles arranged for Mary to marry Joseph, a local carpenter. According to Jewish law, Mary and Joseph were married even though Mary still lived with Anne. Joseph would wait until Mary was old enough to take care of his house before she came to live with him. He planned to welcome Mary into his house soon.

The bride and her friends spent many happy hours getting ready for the wedding. They sewed clothes, wove baskets, and even dried herbs for the bride's kitchen. Mary was in the western meadow gathering mint to dry when Gabriel landed there.

Gabriel folded his wings, looked at Mary, and said, "Mary, you are very special to the Lord, and he is with you."

Mary gasped and stumbled backward, shielding her eyes. I didn't blame her. Gabriel is a magnificent being. He wears a long, silver robe, is surrounded by a glowing light, and his wings reach from his head to his feet. His halo shines as bright as the sun. Gabriel is as impressive on Earth as in heaven.

"Don't be afraid, Mary; God is very pleased with you," Gabriel said.

Mary's shoulders relaxed, but I could smell the fragrance of crushed mint in her hands.

"Mary, you are going to have a baby boy, and you will name him Jesus. He is the son of God, and God will make him a king. His kingdom will never end," Gabriel continued.

Shaking her head, Mary stared at Gabriel and asked, "How can this happen?"

"God will make it happen," Gabriel replied.

As Mary twisted her cloak in her hands, Gabriel told her that her relative, Elizabeth, was going to have a baby. Mary clapped her hands and I heard her whisper, "How wonderful for Elizabeth and Zechariah."

I thought I saw a smile on Gabriel's face when he said, "God can do anything."

Bowing her head, Mary said, "I'm the Lord's servant. May it be as you have said."

Immediately, Gabriel returned to heaven.

Mary stared at the sky, but Gabriel was gone. Walking around the meadow, she raised her hands and began to praise God for noticing her, for blessing her and for... She dropped the crushed mint and sank to the ground, covering her face with her hands.

Mary whispered, "Praise God. O God, please help me. I'm going to have a baby, and I don't have a husband. What do I do now? Why did I come to pick mint by myself? What will people say about me? Will my mother believe me? Will Joseph believe me? O God, no one will believe me. Please help me."

Mary wandered around the meadow, shaking her head and crying. Suddenly, she stopped and smiled. "There is someone who will believe me. Elizabeth will believe me. O God, thank you for giving me a friend who will understand."

Mary hurried home. Her mother was baking bread. "What a wonderful smell," Mary said. "I hope one day my home will smell this good."

"Soon, Mary, very soon," Anne said.

Mary took a deep breath, swallowed hard, and asked, "May I take a trip?"

"Where do you want to go? Why do you want to go? Who will go with you? You know you can't go alone. Mary, I need you here. I don't understand," Anne said as she punched the dough hard.

"I would like to visit Zechariah and Elizabeth. The Judean hills are so pretty this time of year, and the sage smells wonderful. Soon I will be a wife and hopefully a mother; then I won't be able to go visit family. Please let me go before Joseph takes me to his home."

"Mary, Joseph won't be happy with your going away. The talk in the market is that he plans to bring you to his house soon. We will see Elizabeth and

Zechariah when we are in Jerusalem for the next feast. Now, no more of this foolishness."

"Mother, please, let me go now," Mary pleaded.

"Oh, Mary, you aren't making sense ... but if Joseph gives permission, and you can find an escort, I guess you have my permission."

"Oh, thank you. I'll go ask Joseph now."

There was a knock at the door.

"Answer the door, Mary."

"We have come to say goodbye," Speria said as she and Philos entered the house.

"Goodbye? Where are you going?" Anne asked.

"We are going to Hebron to look at some olive groves," Philos answered. "It's been a good year, and I'm thinking about expanding my holdings."

"Could I go with you, please?" Mary asked. "I want to go visit my relatives, and they live near Hebron. I must have an escort or I can't go."

Speria clapped her hands, hugged Mary, and said, "I would love to have company on this journey. Anne, please say yes."

Anne sank down and sighed. "Mary, it looks like you have your escorts. I can't think of two better people than Speria and Philos."

Mary skipped out the door saying, "I have my escorts; now to get Joseph's permission."

Mary had the same conversation with Joseph that she had with Anne. Finally, Joseph said, "Mary, I still don't understand why you want to go all the way to Hebron, but it seems important to you, so you have my permission. Stay close to Philos and Speria until you reach Zechariah's house. Have a nice visit with Elizabeth, and have Zechariah find you a good escort when you come home."

"Thank you, Joseph. You are so good to me," Mary said. "I must go pack; we're leaving in the morning."

I whispered, "Eloooree" as I watched Mary hurry home. Such wonderful things were beginning to happen. Then the shadow of the commander fell across my face.

"Felix, what are you doing?" the commander asked.

"I was watching Gabriel," I replied. "Isn't it wonderful how God is working on planet Earth?"

"Everything God does is wonderful, and it would be wonderful if you would do your work in heaven," the commander growled. "Finish that report before the sun goes down in Nazareth. Tomorrow you will help an old man take his dried apricots to Hebron. His son recently died, and he needs someone to pull the cart to Hebron. The old man does not own a donkey. Get to work, Felix."

"Oh, my aching back," I thought as I clapped my hands to bring up the database.

Road to Hebron

finished my report and proofread and fact checked thousands of entries—at least it seemed like thousands. As soon as the sun came up in Galilee, I yelled, "Eloooree!" and leapt into the cosmos.

I landed behind a hill as a fourteen-year-old boy. I heard groaning and shouting. I peeked over the hill and saw a man with a cartload of dried apricots spilled on the road. "Can I help you?" I called.

"Only if you like apricots and want to walk to Hebron!" he yelled back.

"I love apricots and would enjoy a walk to Hebron," I answered. I scooted down the hill.

"I can't pay you much; no pay until we get to Hebron. I'll feed you on the trip," he said.

"Fine," I said as I reached down and righted the cart. After filling the cart with apricots, we started toward Hebron. I played the part of a donkey. I was in a harness, pulling the cart behind me. My hands grew wet with sweat, and painful blisters formed on my fingers. Finally, we stopped for the night. For dinner, we had apricots and water. I like apricots, but I prefer them with bread or something.

The next day, we joined some other merchants traveling toward Hebron. That night we camped under the stars and had apricots for dinner and breakfast. I was losing my taste for apricots. More travelers joined us including Philos, Speria, and Mary.

I enjoyed traveling with Mary. During the day, she sniffed the wildflowers, sang with the birds, and pointed out the little animals in the rocks as we walked toward Hebron. She laughed and talked with Speria. "Hallelu, hallelu," Mary hummed as she skipped along the dusty road. At night, Speria and Mary cooked for the group, Philos and I drew water from a well, and the other merchants fed the animals. My employer rested. After dinner, we sat around the fire, and Mary sang praises to God. Her beautiful voice will bless her baby.

In the morning, Mary was the first one up. She fixed breakfast and fed the animals. She wanted to be on the road early each day. Most of us trudged along, but Mary skipped. Thanks to Mary and Speria, I didn't eat apricots again on this trip.

One evening, Speria and Mary asked for some water to make a lentil stew. I filled a pot with water and was pouring it into the cookpot. I heard her gasp. "What's wrong?" I asked.

"Your eyes—they have yellow stars in them," she replied. "I don't understand. Where did the stars come from?"

"Maybe it was the fire reflecting in my eyes," I replied, but I knew the truth. I was so excited to be with Mary, the mother of Jesus, that I had let a bit of my angel identity slip out on Earth. Each angel has a color. My color is banana yellow, Philos' is neon green, and Spero's is aqua blue. In heaven we are each surrounded by a halo in our color. On Earth, our color is condensed into a star in our eyes. So, I have a yellow star in each eye, Philos has neon green, and Spero has aqua blue. You must look deep into our eyes to see our stars. I was so excited to be helping Mary that I let a bit of my angelic identity slip out.

Mary gave me a questioning look, but she turned back to make the lentil stew. I kept my distance from Mary for the rest of the trip. I had a hard time controlling my emotions when I was close to the Savior, even if he was a baby in Mary's womb.

Judean Village

L ate one day, we came to the top of a hill, and Mary pointed to a house in a small village below us. "There's Elizabeth's house," she said as she ran down the hill. Philos and Speria dashed after her. Reaching the house, Mary yelled, "Elizabeth! Elizabeth!"

The rest of the group followed Mary into the village. There was a well in the center of town and several nice shade trees; we decided to spend the night there. I wasn't much help setting up camp; I wanted to listen to Mary and Elizabeth.

Elizabeth stepped out of her house and gasped, "Mary, what a blessing to have you and your baby visit me! God is so good to me."

"How did you know?" Mary asked. "I haven't told anyone."

"I just knew. My baby jumped when I saw you, and I just knew," Elizabeth replied.

Mary exclaimed, "Oh, Elizabeth, what a great blessing God is giving you!"

Zechariah came to the door just as Mary began to sing. She praised God for his mercy and power and for keeping his promises. Zechariah grabbed a couple of pottery cutting boards, a reed pen, and some ink, and he wrote down Mary's words.

Later, he copied Mary's song onto parchment. When he gave Mary the parchment, Zechariah wrote in the dirt that she should keep it in a safe place. She rolled it up, tied it with a leather thong, and put it in a linen bag Philos had given her.

The next day, the old man and I continued on to Hebron where we delivered the apricots. My mission over, I returned to heaven. I opened the database to write my report and catch up on the proofreading and fact checking.

"Good to see you working hard, Felix," the commander said. "I've been looking for you because I have a concern. I think you know what it is."

"Yes, sir," I replied. "You're worried about my angelic identity slipping out while I was with Mary."

"Secrecy is an important part of being a Secret Agent Angel. When we look like people, people trust us and we can help them. If we look different, people are afraid and we can't help them. I want you to work with Lt. Parebo on keeping your angelic identity secret. When he says you have improved, you will be assigned missions on Earth again," the commander ordered.

"No, sir, please don't do that," I pleaded.

"Felix, you're one of the best SAAs I have on Earth. Work hard and I'll send you back to Earth as soon as I can. I want you on Earth; you're so caring and kind," the commander said as he walked away.

When I wasn't entering data or working with Lt. Parebo, I watched Mary and Elizabeth. They enjoyed working together: making bread, taking care of the garden, fixing meals, cleaning house, and discussing their blessings—their two miracle boys.

The village rejoiced when Elizabeth gave birth to a son.

I was proofreading and fact checking when the commander approached. "You've been working hard, Felix, and I'm proud of you. Lt. Parebo suggests that you be assigned a trial mission to Earth. You will help a widow drive her sheep to market."

"Thank you, sir!" I yelled. With an "Eloooree!" I was headed to Earth.

I easily found my widow; she had sheep scattered all over the hills near Hebron. As we traveled, I realized that we were near Zechariah's village. I mentioned that there would be a naming ceremony in the next village.

"Is this the baby that was born to the old woman?" the widow asked.

"Yes," I replied. "I think we have time to stop and still get the sheep to market."

"I would like to do that. I want to see this miracle baby," she answered. "Let's go."

"Eloooree!"

She looked at me and shook her head, but into the village we went. I stood at the back of the crowd.

Mary was near Elizabeth, and I didn't want to get too close to her and Jesus.

The rabbi asked, "What do you name this child?"

Everyone looked at Zechariah, but he still couldn't talk. Elizabeth said, "We name our son John."

"John! Why would you name him John?" family and friends shouted. "No one in your family is named John. Zechariah, what do you want to name your son?"

Zechariah stood there nodding his head yes, yes, yes. He grabbed a wax tablet and wrote, "His name is John." Immediately, Zechariah could speak. He yelled over and over, "His name is John! His name is John!"

Zechariah told everyone about Gabriel's visit in the temple. Some people joked about an angel visiting their neighbor; others shook their heads in unbelief. Elizabeth and Mary smiled at Zechariah and nodded yes.

I wanted to stay, but the widow and I had sheep to get to market. I wasn't going to mess up. As soon as the widow sold her sheep, it was Eloooree! flip, flip, flip, and back to heaven.

I entered my report on the widow and her sheep. We got a good price for them. I was trying to stay out of trouble, but I glanced at Earth whenever I had a chance.

Mary and Zechariah discussed their meetings with Gabriel. Mary questioned Zechariah about the prophecies. Would Jesus defeat the Romans? Would he be a king like Herod? Would he be a high priest?

Zechariah shook his head and said, "After all that has happened, Mary, I don't try to predict God; I just trust him, and so should you."

"I do trust him."

"Do you, Mary? Do you really trust him? It's time for you to go home. You must tell Joseph and Anne about your baby," Zechariah said.

"Oh, Zechariah, I'm so scared. What will my mother think of me? What will Joseph think of me?" Mary asked as tears gathered in her eyes.

"Trust in God, Mary," Zechariah said. Elizabeth brushed the tears from Mary's cheek and squeezed her hand.

The next day, Philos and Speria appeared to escort Mary back to Nazareth.

As Mary hugged Elizabeth, the older woman said, "Mary, you have been such a blessing to me. It was hard to have a baby at my age. God knew I needed a young woman to help me with the daily chores. God will take care of you when you speak to Joseph and Anne."

Mary gave a quick nod and then held Elizabeth tighter. Philos eased the two women apart, and Speria wrapped her arm around Mary as they headed out of town.

Nazareth

I glanced toward Earth and saw Mary trudging toward Nazareth. She didn't hum or skip; she didn't even talk to Speria.

The commander was heading toward me. I clapped my hands and started proofreading.

"Good to see you proofreading," the commander said. "But you don't need to proofread the creation story. God wrote it, so we know it's okay."

"Yes, sir," I grimaced. "Sir, may I go comfort Mary?"

"No, Felix. God will take care of Mary," he replied. "Back to work on a recent record."

I proofread a little, watched a little. Watched a bit more, proofread a bit less.

When Nazareth came into view, Mary grabbed Speria's hand. Speria gave Mary a hug. Philos whispered, "Give Anne the great news about Elizabeth first."

"Aren't you coming to my home?" Mary asked. "Aren't you coming with me?"

"No, Mary," Philos said. "We have other business to take care of. God is with you."

"I need you; they will believe you," Mary pleaded, wrapping her shawl tighter around her.

"Just tell the truth, Mary. God will take care of you," Speria encouraged.

Mary stumbled toward Nazareth. Philos and Speria watched her until she entered the town; then they returned to heaven. Philos and Spero joined me, and we watched Mary as she neared her home.

No more proofreading.

Anne heard a noise outside and ran to the door. Mary stood in the yard chewing on her thumb. Anne exclaimed, "Oh, Mary, you're back. I'm so glad you're home. I've missed you so much. Tell me all the news."

Mary grabbed her mother's hands and blurted out, "Elizabeth has a baby boy."

"What! How? She's so old."

"God gave her a boy, a healthy baby boy. Gabriel, the angel, told Zechariah that Elizabeth would have a baby boy. The baby is so cute and strong. Zechariah could not talk the whole time Elizabeth was pregnant. He could only speak after they named the baby John," Mary exploded with good news.

"Mary, please slow down. This is a fantastic story you're telling,"

"Mother, I have more news," Mary said.

"It can't be more exciting than Elizabeth's news," Anne said.

Mary wrapped her arms around her waist, bowed her head, and mumbled, "Mother, I'm pregnant."

"What did you say, Mary?" Anne shouted.

"I'm pregnant," Mary whispered.

"Oh, Mary, how? What happened? What will Joseph think? Who is the father? What will your uncles say? Mary, answer my questions! Now!"

Mary took a deep breath as her mother sank onto a bench. Wiping tears from her cheeks, Mary looked at the floor and said, "God … God is the father."

Anne jerked her head up and glared at Mary. "Mary, stop it. You're in real trouble. Tell me the truth now!"

Mary whispered, "I am telling you the truth. My baby's father is God. Gabriel appeared to me in the western meadow and told me that I would give birth to a son, and that God is his father."

"Gabriel again. Why is God suddenly sending angelic messengers to this family?"

"I don't know. I just know what Gabriel said to me. I'm telling you the truth."

"Oh, Mary, what are we to do? What are you to do?" Anne shouted as she jumped up and paced around the room. "I know I'll invite Joseph to dinner. Tell him the truth. Please don't tell him this story about God being the father of your child. Your only hope is for Joseph to forgive you and still marry you. Please tell him the truth."

Anne started to sob. Mary walked over to hug her, but Anne shook her head no.

Mary left the house and wandered to the western meadow. She called out, "Speria, Philos, where are you?" She received no answer, but a soft breeze caressed her cheek. Spero was gently moving his hand back and forth.

Then she shouted, "Gabriel, I need you. Please come." Gabriel didn't come, but a gray bird with large white wings sang, "Twel Twit Tu, Twel Twit Tu" ("God is with you" in Angelic with a bird accent).

Sinking to the ground, she sobbed out a prayer: "Almighty God, please help me. I am confused; I don't know what to do. May Joseph believe me. May my mother believe me. O God, where are Philos and Speria? Please send Gabriel to help me. Guide me, Almighty God. Help me."

When the sun went down, Mary headed back home and saw Joseph entering Anne's house. With her hand on the door, Mary offered up one more prayer for help and gave the door a push. Anne and Joseph looked up as she entered. A bright smile broke over Joseph's face as he said, "Oh, Mary, I'm glad you're home. I've missed you."

"Hello, Joseph. I hope you are well."

"Anne was telling me about Zechariah's son. What wonderful news! Maybe soon we will have a son," Joseph said.

"Did my mother tell you my news, Joseph?" Mary asked.

"No, I left that news for you," Anne said.

"What news, Mary?" Joseph asked. "Tell me."

Mary took a deep breath, and she looked at her mother and then at Joseph. "I'm pregnant, Joseph," she whispered.

"You're what?" Joseph stared at Mary. "What happened? Who's the father? Tell me now!"

Mary took a couple of steps backward before she said, "God is the father."

"Oh, Mary, please tell the truth. Not this story again," Anne pleaded.

"Mary, tell me the truth!" Joseph demanded.

Mary straightened up, looked at her mother, looked at Joseph, and stated firmly, "I am telling you the truth, and I told my mother the truth. God is the father of my baby. I have I never lied to you. I'm telling you the truth. Oh, why won't someone believe me?"

"I can't believe that," Joseph said. "If you'd told me the truth, I could forgive you. But you tell this wild story; I need a wife I can trust. Anne, I'm sorry; I must break this marriage contract."

As Joseph stormed out of the house, he yelled, "I hope whoever did this to you will take care of you, Mary!"

"He will," Mary stated.

Anne looked at Mary and shook her head. That night I heard two women crying as they lay curled up on their mats.

I continued to watch Mary and Anne. In the middle of the night, a brilliant light covered the two women. When the light lifted, the crying had stopped. Mary and Anne were sleeping peacefully. Philos said, "I remember seeing that light at Mount Sinai with Moses. That was the spirit of God."

"You're right. I remember that light when Solomon dedicated the temple in Jerusalem. God is with Mary and Anne."

"I've got a new assignment," Spero said. He leapt into the cosmos and headed to Earth.

"I need to do my report on my time in Nazareth," Philos said as he clapped his hands to open the database.

I'd better get back to proofreading if I ever hope to get another assignment, I thought. I clapped my hands.

A Carpenter's House

I would sneak a peek at Mary between proofreading and fact checking. Life was hard for her. People realized that Mary was going to have a baby and had no husband. The men of Nazareth called her names. The women of Nazareth refused to talk to her. Everyone bullied her. I wanted to help her, but I was stuck working on the database.

I avoided the commander, but one day he found me sitting in a tree in the Majestic Woods. "Felix, come down. I have a special assignment for you."

"Yes, sir!" I yelled as I jumped down from the tree.

"You are to go to Nazareth and befriend Joseph. He is upset by Mary and won't see his friends. Joseph is to marry Mary. Whatever happens, don't let Joseph break the marriage contract," the commander ordered.

"Yes, sir," I replied. "When do I leave?"

"Now."

Eloooree! leap, and dive toward Nazareth.

I landed outside Nazareth as a traveling merchant selling tools: awls, planes, hammers, nails, etc. I went to Joseph's shop and propped the tools on the wall of the small courtyard in front of his house. This courtyard was his carpentry shop. After selling him a few of my tools, I asked, "When do you plan to marry the widow's daughter? I believe her name is Mary."

"Interesting you should ask," Joseph said. "When you came up, I was going to the rabbi to break the marriage contract."

"Why?" I asked.

"Have you seen her? She's pregnant, and she tells me this wild story that God is the father of her baby!" he shouted. "She had to go see Zechariah and Elizabeth. Why won't she just tell me what happened? Why does she keep repeating this lie?"

"What if it's not a lie? What if Mary is telling the truth?" I asked.

"The truth. Then this would be a once-in-the-history-of-the-world event. No, this whole story is too much to believe," Joseph said as he paced around the courtyard.

"So, you want to break the marriage contract?" I asked.

"Of course; she has ruined both of our lives. I care for her and wanted to marry her. Now I can't believe anything she says!" Joseph shouted as he pushed his work off the bench. "Even if I were willing to marry her, what would people think of me? I would look like a fool. Everyone would laugh at me. No, I can't even think of marrying her."

I remained silent.

Joseph continued, "I checked with the rabbi, and I have two options. I could have Mary stoned to death. I'm not going to do that; I care too much for her, even after all this," Joseph shook his head and sat down on the bench. "My second option is to break the wedding contract. I just walk away from the marriage, and Mary will be alone. In fact, I'm going break the wedding contract now. I'm tired of thinking about it." Joseph started to walk away.

I grabbed his arm. "The sun is almost down; don't bother the rabbi now. Wait until tomorrow. Get a good night's sleep; be certain about your decision. What harm can waiting do?"

Joseph sighed as he sat on his workbench. "I don't know."

"I'll go buy fish and bread. Let's have dinner together," I suggested.

"Well, it's better than eating by myself. I'll get the fire started," Joseph replied. "I can wait until tomorrow."

We ate together, but we didn't speak about Mary again. We went to sleep—Joseph on his roof and I under his olive tree.

Suddenly, Joseph woke me. "I've seen an angel, a real angel. The angel said I should marry Mary. She is telling the truth—her baby's father is God. The baby will be a boy, and we are to name him Jesus. He is the King of kings, the Lord of lords, the Prince of Peace, the Messiah, the Savior. I'm going to get Mary now and bring her home to my house." Joseph was dancing all around me. I was getting dizzy watching him.

"Stop, Joseph," I said. "Let's send word to Anne, so that Mary can be ready when you come. Give Mary a nice wedding celebration."

Joseph shouted, "I don't want to wait that long! I want to see Mary now!"

I grabbed Joseph by his shoulders and looked him in the eye. "Joseph, I'm glad you are excited to wed Mary, but let's make it nice for her. You know that she's had a hard time. You can get the house ready for her, and I will go to the market to buy food for a feast. Then we'll invite your friends to help you escort Mary to her new home. She deserves a nice wedding feast."

Joseph nodded and said, "You're right. I'm off to invite my friends and talk to Anne."

"Joseph, it is the middle of the night. Let's have something to eat and wait until the sun comes up."

"I'll wait until the sunrise, but no longer."

"I'll fix us something to eat."

When the sun peeked over the horizon, Joseph and I walked into Nazareth. Joseph was going to Anne's, and I was going to the market. We stopped at the potter's house and the weaver's house to tell them the good news. The men nodded but didn't promise to come to the wedding.

I listened as Joseph entered Anne's yard. She was picking grapes. He said, "Great news, Anne. Mary is telling the truth. God is the father of her baby. An angel came to me last night and told me to marry your daughter. I'm coming back this evening to escort Mary to my home."

"Oh, Joseph, how can I ever thank you? You are good to take Mary as your wife. May God bless you."

"May God forgive me for not believing Mary. Thanks be to God for sending his angel to me. Have Mary ready this evening; try to get a couple of Mary's friends to join her."

"May God forgive us both. We'll be ready, and I'll convince some friends to join us."

As I returned from the market, I saw Mary in the western meadow. I stopped to watch. Mary ran to the mint patch where she held her hands up and shouted, "Thank you, God! Thank you for being so gracious to me. What a wonderful God you are. Thank you and all glory to you. Amen."

I whispered, "Eloooree!"

Mary headed back to her house.

I continued to Joseph's house. Normally, the women in Joseph's life would fix the feast, but they were ashamed of Mary. They refused to cook a wedding feast for her, so I would. SAAs can do whatever needs to be done.

Joseph was busy straightening up his home when I returned from the market. We started roasting the lamb.

"Ah! The lamb smells wonderful!" Joseph exclaimed.

I laughed. "That's your excitement talking. It hasn't been cooking long enough to smell. Wait until you taste the lentil stew; I make it spicy. In addition to the lentil stew and the lamb, we're having unleavened bread; a salad of mint, parsley, green onion, thyme, and celery with olive oil dressing; plus fig cakes and almonds. I have a special treat for Mary and you: oranges."

"I need to get the banquet table ready," Joseph said as he shook and beat his rugs and laid them on the ground under the olive tree. The scent of olive blossoms filled the air. The guests would sit on the rugs and use flat unleavened bread as both plate and spoon. Food would be scooped out of large dishes set in the middle of the blankets.

Just before sundown, Joseph took a bath and changed into his wedding clothes. He wore a beige sleeveless cotton tunic and a brown striped woolen robe tied with a braided belt. When he signed the contract to wed Mary, Joseph bought these clothes for his wedding. He showed me his new clothes, his freshly trimmed beard, and the wooden necklace he had made for Mary.

As we walked down the street, he asked his friends to join him. A few did; most didn't.

Joseph knocked on the door to Anne's house and requested that Mary come to his house. Anne pulled back a curtain covering the back half of the house. Joseph broke into a big smile when he saw Mary in a white cotton tunic and a light grey wool robe tied with a white wool belt. She wore a white veil over her face held in place by a metal band holding a few coins. The coins were her treasure, her money. Joseph whispered, "She is the most beautiful woman I have ever seen!"

Her friends led her to Joseph. He took Mary's hand and whispered, "Forgive me, Mary, for not believing you." Mary squeezed his hand and smiled.

Two escorts picked up a small chest containing the items Mary was bringing to her new home: a few pottery bowls, an oil lamp, some baskets, a rug

Mary had woven, and a few cooking utensils plus dried herbs. Joseph led Mary to his house, followed by the rest of the wedding party. Many neighbors watched, but they didn't join in the celebration.

This was not the wedding that Mary or Joseph had expected, so many friends were missing. Joseph and Mary drank from a wedding cup and sat together under their olive tree. The small wedding party enjoyed the wedding feast. One of Joseph's friends played his flute, a couple of Mary's friends danced with their tambourines, and Mary sang from Song of Solomon. Joseph smiled. Eloooree!!

Nazareth

I was in the Reflection Grotto fact checking records when I felt a tingle. I pulled up the hologram to see what my mission was. Roman taxes were due, and Joseph didn't have enough money to pay them. I was to order a table. The payment for the table would pay the taxes. I yelled, "Eloooree!" and leapt into the cosmos.

I entered the front courtyard of Joseph's one-room house. He hurried to greet me. "Shalom. How may I help you?" he asked.

"I need a table, and I need it soon. Can you make one by next week?" I answered.

"Yes, I would be glad to," Joseph said. "Please have a seat."

"Your olive tree has fruit very early this year," I said as I sat on a bench in the shade of the olive tree.

"Yes, we have so many olives that we have sold them to my wife's uncles. The tree just keeps producing olives; it's a miracle."

"God is good."

Joseph went to the door of his house and called, "Mary, please bring some water and figs for our guest. We are discussing a table he needs."

Mary appeared, holding a wooden tray with a pitcher of water and two cups plus a dish of figs. "Please have some water; the figs are from our tree in the back. I will give you some grapes from the vine on the back wall when you leave," Mary said.

"Thank you very much. What sweet figs," I replied.

"More miracles," Joseph said. "The figs are plentiful this year, and the chickens are laying dozens of eggs. The clusters of grapes are huge and juicy. Our harvest is better than anyone else in Nazareth. Now, back to business. What type of table do you want?"

Joseph and I completed our business, and I paid him for the table. As I walked away, I looked back to see him climbing the stairs on the side of the house. He knelt on the roof to pray. I continued to walk down the road and out of Nazareth. Roman soldiers entering Nazareth marched past me.

Outside Nazareth, I walked behind a tree and yelled, "Eloooree!" I then did three flips and headed back to heaven. From there, I checked on Mary and Joseph.

Joseph looked toward the center of Nazareth. "Mary, bad news. Roman soldiers are in town. They never bring good news!" Joseph yelled. "I'll go see what's happening."

Joseph hurried to the center of town. A soldier was reading a decree from the emperor: "Everyone must be counted. You must go to your family's city and enter your names on the tax rolls there. This is the emperor's command, and you must not delay obeying it."

Joseph rushed home to tell Mary the news. "I'm from the family of David; I must go to Bethlehem."

"The baby is coming soon; I can't walk to Bethlehem. Please stay in Nazareth until after the baby is born," Mary pleaded.

"I don't think the Romans will allow me to wait that long. While I make the table, we'll pray for God to provide a donkey for you to ride to Bethlehem. If we don't have a donkey by the time the table is finished, I must go to Bethlehem without you," Joseph said.

I sat down, clapped my hands, and thought about Joseph. Joseph's record appeared in front of me. Joseph earned five stars for this visit—one for honesty, one for generosity, one for hospitality, one for gratitude, and one for industry. As I was closing the record, Lt. Parebo sat down beside me.

"Good work," he said. "I've got special instructions for your next mission. You're going on a road trip. Here's a map. At the first stop, you'll buy a small herd of donkeys. At the second stop, you'll get a cart of salted fish. Then head to Nazareth. You'll know what to do in Nazareth."

"When do I go?"

"Now, and don't dawdle," Lt. Parebo said.

"Yes, sir," I replied. Walking all over Galilee was much better than proofreading. I grabbed my map and headed to Earth.

Soon I was heading into Nazareth with my donkeys and fish when the axle on the cart broke and confusion exploded.

CRACK, CRASH, HE-HAW, HE-HAW, STOP, STOP!!!

The cart turned over, spilling its load of fish. Frightened donkeys brayed and bolted. I yelled and ran after the donkeys. People ran to pick up the fish.

After I rounded up the donkeys, I asked, "Where can I find a carpenter?"

Someone pointed to Joseph's house. I walked into the front courtyard and asked Joseph if he could fix my cart. Joseph didn't recognize me. I was a young man with brown hair today. When I ordered the table earlier, I was an older man with grey hair.

"Of course, I can fix it," Joseph replied.

"I have one problem," I said. "I won't have any money to pay for the repairs until I return from selling the fish and the donkeys in Jerusalem. Can you wait until then?"

"That's not how we do business around here; you should pay for the repairs when they are done," Joseph answered, "but we may be able to work out a deal. I'll repair your cart if I can borrow one of the donkeys for a month. Because of the emperor's decree, I must go to Bethlehem, and I need to take my wife with me."

I pointed to one of the donkeys. "If you can fix my cart today, I'll give you that donkey. He is gentle; your wife will have a smooth ride."

Joseph grinned. "It's a deal. You must have been sent by God."

I nodded and said, "Yes."

Joseph just stared at me, and then he ran to his house. "Mary, I have good news: God sent us a donkey." Grabbing his tools, Joseph headed down the street to get to work.

Mary came outside and invited me to sit under the olive tree. She offered me a dipper of water and some large, juicy grapes. "Rest and refresh," Mary said.

"So, you're going to Bethlehem," I said.

"Yes, I've never been there; have you?" Mary answered.

"King David was from there. The prophet Micah tells us that the Savior will be born in Bethlehem. It's a very special place."

"So that's why we must go to Bethlehem," Mary mumbled. Then she smiled at me and said, "Rest in the shade and get more water if you wish. I must go pack for our trip."

I sat down and let out a sigh when Mary went inside. I was struggling to keep my angel identity hidden. It was difficult for me to be so close to Jesus and Mary.

Joseph fixed the axle, and I gave him the donkey. While I loaded up my cart and tied the donkeys together, I watched Joseph. He fed the donkey straw and gave him water. Mary rubbed the donkey's velvet ears and laughed, "I like this donkey. I'm going to name him Micah."

"Micah—that's an interesting name for a donkey," Joseph said.

"It's a good name," Mary said. "Micah said the Savior would be born in Bethlehem."

I returned to heaven and wrote another five-star report on Joseph for industry, kindness, creativity, gratitude, and humility. I watched the couple prepare for their journey.

Joseph took grapes and olives plus the chickens to Anne.

"I want to go with you, Joseph, but my knees can't make that long trip," Anne said.

"I'll take good care of Mary, and we'll be home before you've had time to miss us," Joseph answered.

Mary packed bread, figs, and salted fish (a gift from me) to eat on the journey.

The warmth and light of the sunrise woke Joseph. He stretched and gave Mary a gentle shake. "Time to get up. The sun is up, and we should be, too. I'll take care of the donkey; you finish packing."

Mary groaned as she stood up. "I'll get some bread and raisins for breakfast. I want to get started before the day gets too hot."

Joseph put a halter around the donkey's neck and tied blankets on his back. He looked at Mary and said, "Now you can ride in comfort."

Mary pushed some long strips of cloth between the blankets; she planned to wrap the baby in these strips when he was born. Joseph lifted Mary onto the donkey and they left Nazareth. Soon they joined the crowds of people traveling south.

Bethlehem

I sat down to do some fact checking when the Celestial Choir began to sing a new song. I smiled as I clapped to open the database. Even fact checking couldn't ruffle me today. I was content to read and listen, listen and read. A tingle interrupted my peace. I pulled up a hologram of an inn in Bethlehem. I was to rent the last spot in this inn and clean its stable. Phew, but orders are orders. Off to Bethlehem I went.

As I entered the Earth's atmosphere, I looked around. Joseph, Mary, and Micah were slowly climbing the hills around Bethlehem. I landed outside Bethlehem and walked into town in the form of a Galilean peasant arriving for the census.

I checked the inns in town. All I heard was "No vacancy, no room, no vacancy." I knocked on the door of a rundown inn and asked if there was a sleeping spot available.

"Hope you only need one spot," the innkeeper said. "I could squeeze you in here by the door. People will hit you as they go in and out, but it's the best you're going to do."

"It'll do," I said as I looked around the inn. It was crowded, noisy, dark, and smelly. Men were drinking and gambling in the corner; their shouts echoed through the room. Children ran around laughing and jumping.

"God, please protect us from a fire if an oil lamp is knocked over," I whispered.

Women talked and cooked outside. Their spicy stew smelled delicious. I don't need food, but some of these people looked as if they could use a good meal. "God, may they share with the hungry," I prayed.

"Would you mind if I cleaned your stable?" I asked the innkeeper. "I like to stay busy."

"If that's how you have fun, fine with me," the innkeeper replied. "I doubt it's been cleaned in months, but there will be no reduction in the cost of your sleeping spot."

My nose led me to the stable and its awful smell. I put the sheep and a cow in an outside enclosure. Every surface in the stable was scrubbed, rubbed, or scraped. I combed the sheep until their coats were soft and fluffy. I washed the cow until it smelled like lilies—well, maybe like a cow in a field full of lilies. I put out fresh hay and water and left a couple of lamps on a shelf. The stable was cleaner, smelled better, and was warmer than the inn. If I was staying, I would sleep there, not the inn.

My mission was finished, so I went to pay the innkeeper. KNOCK, KNOCK, KNOCK. I opened the door. There stood Joseph and Mary; they looked exhausted.

The innkeeper glanced at them and said, "Sorry, the inn is full."

Now I knew why I cleaned the stable. I suggested, "They could stay in the stable; it's clean."

The innkeeper grunted, "If they wish, they can stay in the stable tonight for half price."

Joseph gave a weak smile and said, "Thank you."

I led Joseph and Mary to the stable. Joseph spread out his cloak and Mary lay down on it. I brought hay and water to Micah. I offered to get some stew for them, and Joseph nodded his head yes.

While I waited for the stew, I said to the man next to me, "The Savior, the Messiah, will be born in Bethlehem, maybe tonight. Praise God."

He laughed at me and said, "How foolish! Everyone knows that the Messiah will be born in Jerusalem in a palace."

Another man said, "The Savior won't be born at all; he will just appear with an army to defeat the Romans."

"Remember Micah's prophecy; he said the Messiah would be born in Bethlehem," I replied.

"Those old prophets—what did they know? I think God has forgotten us," another man stated.

"God hasn't forgotten!" I shouted, but the men just laughed and started playing dice.

Grabbing two bowls of stew, I hurried to Joseph. He took the bowls, and my mission was over. I walked over a hill to return to heaven when I felt a tingle and pulled up a hologram of shepherds on the outskirts of Bethlehem.

I hurried to the hills outside town. Shepherds dozed while their sheep slept. I wondered if I should wake them up or let them sleep. If I woke them up, what would I say to them?

While I thought about what to do, I noticed the sky was getting lighter. One star seemed to be coming closer and closer and closer. It wasn't a star; it was an angel—a herald angel. I gazed in wonder, but the shepherds were face down and shaking in fear.

I ran to reassure them when the herald angel said, *"Don't be afraid. I have some very good news for you—news that will make everyone happy. Today your Savior was born in David's town. He is the Messiah, the Lord. This is how you will know him: You will find a baby wrapped in pieces of cloth and lying in a feeding box."* [1]

Suddenly, the sky was as light as day as the Celestial Choir filled the sky. They praised God singing, *"Praise God in heaven, and on earth let there be peace to the people who please him."* [2]

I knew this song. The Celestial Choir had been singing it. All nature rejoiced with the angels. The stars sparkled brighter, the moon glowed like a comet, and the wind whistled a happy tune. Too soon, the angels returned to heaven, and Earth became quiet.

The shepherds were amazed. They began debating: "Do you suppose it is true?" "Should we leave the sheep and go find out?" "Why would God tell us?" "How will we find the baby in Bethlehem?" "Bethlehem is so crowded, we'll never find this baby. Let's just stay here."

"I know where the baby is," I said.

The shepherds looked at me.

"Who are you?"

"How to do you know where the baby is?"

"This is more exciting than watching sheep. Let's go," the lead shepherd said.

The shepherds followed me as we hurried through the dark streets of Bethlehem. My heart was pounding in my chest. I was bringing people to Jesus.

"Here it is!" I yelled as I pointed to the run-down inn.

"The Messiah, the Savior, is in there?" one shepherd asked. "My shepherd's hut is better than that!"

"No, in the stable," I said. "Over there."

"That's worse."

"There's a light in the stable!" one shepherd shouted.

The stable door creaked as they eased it open. Sitting in the light of two lamps, a woman sang softly to a newborn baby. The baby was wrapped in strips of cloth and was lying in a feeding box as the angel had said. The shepherds slipped in and knelt down.

The shepherds told Joseph and Mary about the angel and the angelic chorus, about the glory and the majesty, and how they were directed to the stable. Mary snuggled her baby close when she realized her son's birth was proclaimed in the heavens.

I slipped in and looked at Joseph first. He looked tired and puzzled. Then my eyes moved to Mary. She was tired but happy. I looked at the baby, at Jesus.

Mary gasped, "Yellow stars from the road to Hebron. I know you."

I ran from the stable, through the town, and into the hills surrounding Bethlehem. Tears of joy, tears of embarrassment, or tears of disappointment streamed from my eyes. I had to get back to heaven. Eloooree! but I had the energy to do only one flip—not enough thrust to break through Earth's atmosphere. Backward, backward, I fell until I landed in a cold, damp bog. SLURP, SPLASH, SLURP, SPLASH. I walked out of the bog and onto solid ground. Eloooree! flip, flip, flip, and zoom toward heaven. I had forgotten to adjust my directional indicator and landed in the middle of the Lord's Army.

The Lord's Army was celebrating the birth of the Savior, the Messiah, by chanting Elbildo (Angelic for "God's will be done"). The Archangel Michael yelled, "El!" and the soldiers yelled back, "Bildo!" I joined in for a couple of chants, but the soldiers gave me a "Who are you?" look. Elbildo is their thing, so I headed back to Meditation Point and the other SAAs.

All heaven was rejoicing over the birth. The cherubim zipped through heaven trailing streams of color behind them. Heaven was filled with loops and whorls of color. The seraphim surrounded God's throne singing, "Merciful, Merciful, Merciful," not their usual song of "Holy, Holy, Holy." God is both merciful and holy, so both songs were correct. The Celestial Choir continued to sing, "Praise God in heaven, and on earth let there be peace to the people who please him." How were the SAAs celebrating Jesus' birth?

As I approached Mediation Point, I heard shouts of "Eloooree! Eloooree!" Then I saw SAAs flipping and jumping. I did a triple flip and a double somersault. Time is different in heaven than on Earth. In heaven we don't have time—no days, no hours, and no years. I don't know how long we celebrated.

When I saw the commander coming toward me, I stopped halfway through a quad twirl. No point in trying to hide now. I walked up and said, "I'm sorry, sir. I was just so excited when I saw God among the people."

"Felix, you must learn to control your angelic emotions, especially on Earth. I'm taking you off Earth missions for a while. Lt. Parebo and you will figure out ways to keep your angelic identity hidden," the commander said. "I need you on Earth. You work so well with people. I am relieving you of proofreading and fact checking while you work with Lt. Parebo. Work hard, Felix, work hard. I need you."

"Yes, sir," I said.

"Stay here. Lt. Parebo is on his way," the commander said as he walked toward Spero.

The commander said something to Spero, and they both looked at me. Spero nodded his head, yelled, "Eloooree!" and leapt into the cosmos. I watched as

Spero, a vegetable seller in the Bethlehem market, introduced Joseph to a widow. This mission should have been mine, but I messed up and Spero got it.

Joseph and the widow agreed that he, Mary, and Jesus could stay with her. Joseph would repair the house, and Mary would help with cooking and cleaning. Joseph hurried away to get Mary and Jesus. The widow hurried home to straighten up. Spero folded up his stall and hurried back to heaven.

Lt. Parebo walked up, and that was the last time I saw Earth for I don't know how many Earth months.

Later I heard that the widow and Mary enjoyed being together. Joseph did plenty of repairs for the widow, but he also did other work. Joseph and Mary decided to stay in Bethlehem a little longer. They had a comfortable life there. Eventually they would go back to Nazareth, but not right away. They would wait until God directed them.

Susa

One day, Lt. Parebo said to me, "Felix, you have so much joy in you. We need a way for you to let out some of that joy without letting out your angelic identity. Do you have any ideas of what you could do?"

"Maybe I could leap or flip when I feel so joyful that I might lose control," I answered.

"This is to be a solution for the long term, and I think flipping around might be distracting in many cases," Lt. Parebo answered. "What do you think about snapping your fingers?"

"I have a hard time snapping my fingers," I replied. "I could clap my hands."

"Many people clap their hands to summon servants. Clapping hands could cause confusion," Lt. Parebo answered. "What about something not so physical, like humming?"

"Wouldn't that be disturbing? What would I hum?" I asked.

"You could hum loudly or softly. I was thinking you could hum the song the seraphim sing, '*Holy, Holy, Holy,*'" Lt. Parebo said.

"I could hum loudly when in a crowd or to myself when in a small group. I love the song. This might work," I said.

"Good, we'll start practicing tomorrow," Lt. Parebo said. "You're working hard, Felix. Way to go."

An Earth month later, I was practicing my humming when the commander said, "Lt. Parebo says you are doing well, so I have decided to send you on a mission."

"Thank you, sir. Thank you!" I shouted as I did a double flip. "When do I go?"

"Don't you want to know where you're going and why?"

"Oh, yes, sir," I answered as I did another flip.

"This is a test mission. During part of the mission, you will be close to Jesus, and you must keep your angelic identity secret. Philos and Spero will be nearby when you are close to Jesus. They can give you support," the commander explained.

"I can keep my identity secret without their help," I snapped.

"Felix, if you fail, you won't go back to Earth until Jesus has left Earth. I don't know how long Jesus will be there—a year, ten, or a hundred. I just don't know. Take all the help you can get," the commander replied.

"Yes, sir," I mumbled.

"You're going to Susa in Persia. God has placed a new star in the sky to announce the birth of Jesus. You'll help a wise man in Persia understand the meaning of this star. Spero and Philos have similar missions. Spero is going to Sana in Arabia, and Philos is going to Bharuch on the coast of India."

"I'll do my best, sir," I replied.

"I'm counting on it," the commander answered. "Pull up the hologram of the man you'll be helping, and then off you go."

Eloooree! flip, flip, flip, zoom.

After landing, I headed to the nearest tavern to look for my wise man. According to the hologram, he was about thirty, was well-dressed, and had a neatly trimmed black beard. I ordered a cup of honeyed water and observed the men sitting at the tables. The men in the corner had on dusty worn clothes, and the ones by the door had long scraggly beards. Two men in the center were dressed like servants. I must be in the wrong tavern. As I started to leave, I heard one of the servants say, "Without his assistant, Vaumisa is going to have a hard time translating those Jewish manuscripts. He doesn't speak Hebrew."

I eased onto a bench near these men; they may know my wise man.

"I can't decide if Vaumisa is brilliant or a dreamer. He thinks he has found a new star in the sky," the other servant said.

These men know my wise man. "Excuse me, I couldn't help overhearing," I said. "Maybe I can help your master."

"You shouldn't listen to private conversations," one servant replied.

"I doubt it you can help Vaumisa," the other servant said. "Our master needs someone who is familiar with the religion of the Jews."

"I have spent time in Judea and speak the languages of the region," I replied. "I have just arrived in Susa and need a job. Would you introduce me to your master?"

"It couldn't hurt. Come with me."

We left the tavern together, and soon I was speaking with a well-dressed, thirty-four-year-old man with a neatly trimmed black beard. Vaumisa was my wise man.

"Is it true that you can speak Aramaic, Hebrew, Greek, and Latin?" he asked.

"Yes, and I am familiar with the Hebrew religion," I replied.

"I'll give you a try. You can begin by translating these Hebrew writings I recently bought from a trader in Africa," Vaumisa said as he handed me two scrolls. I recognized them from my time in Africa. "Tonight, you will join me on the roof to take notes on my observations of the night sky."

"Thank you, sir."

Vaumisa was the third son of the regional governor. His oldest brother worked in the government. The second brother was a general in the army. Vaumisa was a scholar and priest. His library contained scrolls written in Persian, Hebrew, Greek, and even Hindi. The scrolls covered many topics—including science, religion, and history—but his main interest was astronomy.

Every night we went to the roof of his home to study the stars. He believed the new star announced a change in the universe.

One night, I handed Vaumisa his astrolabe, an instrument used to mark the positions of stars and other celestial bodies. After looking at the star, Vaumisa said, "Felix, look how brilliant this star is. It outshines all the other stars in the universe."

"You are right, sir. It's glorious," I replied.

"All the stars in the sky move; this one doesn't," Vaumisa said. "The sky is a treasure map, and this star is marking the birthplace of a special king."

"I agree with you, sir," I replied. "We should follow this treasure map you found."

"You're right, Felix. Let's go on a treasure hunt. Let's meet this king. I'll make arrangements, and you begin packing the equipment and supplies we'll need."

"Yes, sir," I said. "Eloooree!" I whispered.

"What?" Vaumisa called out as he walked away.

"Nothing, sir."

Soon we were ready to travel to Judea. Our caravan consisted of camels, horses, and donkeys. The camels were for Vaumisa and his scientific and personal supplies, including his favorite treat: sugared almonds. I rode in a cart drawn by a donkey so I could continue my work. I was offered a camel, but writing while balanced on a camel's rocking hump is hard. Soldiers traveled on horses, and servants and entertainers rode in carts or walked. Other carts were filled with supplies. Shortly after sunrise, our caravan headed west from Susa to the Euphrates River and then on to Jerusalem.

Jerusalem

*O*ur caravan entered the Roman Empire, the greatest country at that time. King Herod ruled Judea, a province of the empire, and had a palace in Jerusalem. Caesar Augustus was emperor and King Herod was like a governor of a state in the empire.

Vaumisa wanted to meet King Herod and ask him about the new King of the Jews. This was a bad idea. King Herod was dangerous and would be angry about another king in Judea. I must be alert and keep Vaumisa safe.

We set up camp outside Jerusalem. People admired the large tents, smelled the incense, and listened to the musicians. The large white and gold silk dining canopy echoed the glory of the temple. Vaumisa burned incense made of dried rose petals and mint every day. It reminded him of the perfume his wife wore. Musicians played harps and drums at every meal.

King Herod could not ignore our large camp. His soldiers asked Vaumisa why he had come to Jerusalem. Vaumisa gave them a letter from his father, the governor of Susa. The letter requested a visit with the king of the Jews. King Herod was delighted that we had come so far to visit him, a king of the Jews. He invited Vaumisa to a banquet at the palace that night.

"Herod is the wrong king of the Jews. Isn't he?" Vaumisa asked me.

"He is not the one we seek. King Herod is known as Herod the Great, but I don't agree. Herod the Evil is a better name for him. He will do anything to stay in power, including killing members of his own family," I answered.

"He must be called 'great' for a reason," Vaumisa said.

"Herod has done one good thing: he built the beautiful temple in Jerusalem," I replied as I gazed at the white and gold temple in the center of Jerusalem.

"I will say we are too tired to come to a banquet tonight, but we would enjoy dining with King Herod after we have rested," Vaumisa said.

King Herod agreed to delay the banquet for three days.

The next day, Spero and his master Amjad arrived from Sana in Arabia. Their camp was as big and grand as ours. They had traveled from the tip of Arabia up along the Red Sea and across to Jerusalem. Amjad and his soldiers rode on majestic horses. The people watched the horses train and race. Some soldiers rode standing on the back of a horse. One soldier rode standing on the back of two horses. Every boy in Jerusalem came to watch the horses.

Herod's soldiers questioned Amjad about why he was in Jerusalem. Amjad replied, "I desire to see the king of the Jews, for I have heard so much about him. I hope he will see me."

Herod was delighted with Amjad's answer and invited him to the banquet in two days.

Amjad was the fourth son of the king in Sana. He was a scholar, a star gazer, and a warrior. That night, Amjad and Spero ate with us. The wise men discussed their discovery of a new star and its meaning.

The third day, Akash from Bharuch on the Indian coast and Philos arrived in Jerusalem. They had sailed the Arabian Sea to the Persian Gulf. Then they traveled over land to Jerusalem. Akash had several elephants carrying their supplies.

The captain of the soldiers spotted Akash as soon as he arrived in Jerusalem. "Why have you come to Jerusalem?" the captain asked. "Are you spies or are you plotting against the Romans?"

Akash waved his hand at them and said, "Of course not. I want to see the king of the Jews. I saw his special star in the sky. Where can I find him?"

A third grand caravan puzzled Herod. When he heard about the special star, Herod became upset. Why had these caravans arrived in Jerusalem? Herod wanted—no, needed—to know what was happening. He would find out at the banquet.

Big crowds came to see the elephants. The people of Jerusalem were familiar with camels and horses, but elephants were special. The elephants set up the tents and even saluted King Herod. Water was provided so the elephants could cool off by spraying water in the air. All day the squeals of the children of Jerusalem were heard as they got sprayed by the elephants.

Akash was a star gazer and a merchant. He owned a fleet of ships and traded with Africa, Arabia, and Asia. As he traveled, he purchased rare and ancient writings, trying to determine the meaning of life. Among his manuscripts were the Jewish prophecies about a special king. He had taken this long journey hoping to find this king.

Amjad hosted a banquet for Vaumisa and Akash. They ate little, but they talked all night about this new king of the Jews. They hoped Herod could tell them exactly where this new king was. Spero, Philos, and I looked at each other. Herod had many spies and knew many secrets, but he did not know where this king was, and we needed to keep it that way.

Herod threw a grand banquet the next night with our masters as guests of honor. All the powerful men of Jerusalem were there. We ate roast peacock with all the trimmings. While we ate, musicians played flutes, harps, and tambourines. Actors with elaborate masks put on skits. Dancers twirled and leapt around the banquet hall. Acrobats performed elaborate flips, somersaults, and handstands.

Everyone was enjoying the lavish feast until Akash asked, "Where is the newborn king of the Jews? We saw his star and have come to worship him."

The room became silent as everyone looked at Herod. He rose from his red velvet couch and strode to the table where Akash was reclining. Herod slammed his fists on the table and glared at Akash. Amjad and Vaumisa walked toward Akash with their hands on the hilts of their daggers. Herod's soldiers drew their swords. Philos, Spero, and I offered up a prayer. Taking a deep breath, Herod stared at Amjad and Vaumisa and asked, "Did you see this star, too?"

They nodded their heads yes.

"Please, tell us where the king of the Jews was born," Vaumisa asked.

"I don't know, but my scholars will search for the answer," Herod said. "Please return to the palace at noon, and I will have the answer then."

The scholars hurried away to begin searching prophecies for an answer. The other guests scurried away, glad to have avoided Herod's fury.

Early the next morning, a messenger from Herod brought a note to Amjad, Akash, and Vaumisa. The note requested that they come to the palace right away. Our masters and Philos, Spero, and I followed the messenger to Herod's palace. We did not take a direct way, but we went through underground tunnels and secret passages. We stopped in front of a large wooden door. The messenger tapped, tapped, tapped, tapped, tapped, tapped, tapped on the door. We heard Herod yell, "Away everyone! I need privacy."

The messenger eased the door open, and we stepped into Herod's private office. King Herod and we were the only ones in the office.

"Welcome, my friends. I hope you slept well last night," Herod said.

"We did," Akash answered. "I hope you are well this morning."

"Have your scholars determined where the king of the Jews was born?" Amjad asked.

"I will answer that question at the public visit at noon," Herod said.

Amjad looked at Vaumisa; Vaumisa looked at Akash; Akash looked at Amjad.

"I have a question for you," Herod said. "When did you first see this star?"

"About a year ago," Vaumisa said.

"Do you two agree?" Herod asked.

Amjad and Akash nodded yes.

"Wonderful. Come back at noon, and I will have the answer to your question," Herod said.

"Could you tell us now?" Akash asked.

"At noon," Herod said and left his office. The messenger guided us back through the secret passages and the underground tunnels.

"What was the meaning of all that?" Amjad asked. Vaumisa and Akash just shrugged.

"What was Herod planning?" I wondered. "It would be bad."

At noon we returned to Herod's palace, but by the normal route.

"Good to see you," Herod said. "Hope you had a good morning."

"We had an interesting morning," Vaumisa said.

"Can you tell us where the king of the Jews was born?" Akash asked.

"He was born in Bethlehem," Herod said. "It is a town not far from Jerusalem. I cannot leave Jerusalem at this time, but I can send someone to guide you."

"That's not necessary. My secretary knows the area well. Thank you for getting the information so quickly," Vaumisa answered. "With your permission, we will go to Bethlehem today."

"Of course, you have my permission. Please return to Jerusalem and tell me where this king of the Jews is. I want to worship him," Herod commanded.

Spero, Philos, and I looked at each other. Herod could not be trusted. We must not allow our masters to return to Jerusalem.

Most of Jerusalem lined the road as we left town. Akash led the way. His elephants wore bright headdresses and blankets decorated with emeralds, rubies, and diamonds on their backs. Each elephant used his trunk to hold the tail of the one in front of him. Amjad came next. He and his men rode in gold and silver chariots drawn by horses with red and blue plumes in their manes. The soldiers entertained the crowd by driving their chariots in circles and figure eights. Vaumisa came last, riding his camels with tassels and bells hanging from their harnesses and humps. Each time they took a step, everyone heard "ting-a-ling, ting-a-ling." Our masters threw nuts and dates to the children who ran alongside the caravan. We made quite an impression on Jerusalem.

Bethlehem

We arrived in Bethlehem at sunset. The streets were too narrow for the animals to pass, so we camped outside the city. Looking over the city, our masters wondered where they would find the baby king.

"Let's go to the center of the town and speak with the leaders," Vaumisa said. "Surely they'll know where he is."

"I don't want to spend time with politicians and business leaders. The king of the Jews is going to live in the biggest house. Let's go there," Amjad reasoned.

"I don't know. This king is different; he may not live in a big house. Let's ask at the market who has a one-year-old baby boy," Akash suggested.

That night as the wise men looked at the stars, the special star appeared over a house.

"Our star is telling us!" Akash yelled.

"We know where the child is!" Vaumisa exclaimed.

"Praise God for showing us the way!" Amjad shouted.

Early the next morning, our masters went to a small house on a narrow street in Bethlehem. Joseph was outside working on a bench. He was astonished when elegantly dressed noblemen walked into the courtyard.

"My dear carpenter, where can we find the king of the Jews?" Vaumisa asked.

"The king of the Jews is Herod, and he lives in the palace in Jerusalem," Joseph replied.

"We know about that king of the Jews; he's not the one we are seeking," Amjad stated. He then explained about the meeting with Herod.

Joseph looked concerned. Mary came out of the house holding Jesus.

"My soul tells me he is the king of the Jews!" Akash exclaimed. Vaumisa, Amjad, and Akash dropped to their knees to worship Jesus. Mary and Joseph were bewildered, but Jesus held Mary's robe and looked peaceful. Mary stroked his dark, curly hair and reached for his chubby hand. Jesus smiled as he looked up at his mother.

I felt a rush of joy and my knees started to bend. Spero pushed me behind Philos. "Felix, your stars are showing," Spero whispered.

I took a deep breath and closed my eyes. I hummed to myself until I felt in control. To be certain no angelic identity was showing, I tapped Philos on the shoulder. He looked at me, smiled, and mouthed, "Doing great."

Moving over behind Vaumisa, I glanced at Jesus. Spero nodded his head and gave me a thumbsup signal. I wanted to flip and leap; my angelic emotions were under control. I had done it. The humming had worked.

Joseph said, "Come into the house quickly!"

A large crowd was gathering in the street. Joseph knew Herod had spies everywhere. It would be dangerous if Herod found out that these wealthy and important men had come to a small home on tiny street. Our masters decided to keep one soldier at the house and send the servants back to the caravans for food and gifts.

Ten adults and one child squeezed into the small house. Everyone sat on the dirt floor. The soldier sat near the door. The wise men were in the center of the room, and we sat behind them. Joseph sat where he could see the door and the visitors. Mary and the widow were in the corner making bread. Jesus crawled around visiting everyone.

Servants returned with food and gifts, and everyone enjoyed a meal of roasted lamb, raisin cakes, olive oil, and bread. Amjad brought some giant dates from Sana. Akash provided dried mangoes. Vaumisa shared his sugared almonds.

Mary and Joseph told the story of Jesus' birth. Our masters asked about the dreams, the angels, and the prophecies. They talked long into the night. I think they would have stayed all night, but Jesus went to sleep in Mary's lap. The widow fell asleep in the corner. Mary's head nodded, and Joseph yawned. Our masters stood up to go.

"I have a gift for the child," Vaumisa said. He handed Joseph a green velvet bag full of gold coins. Joseph gasped in amazement when he looked in the bag. These gold coins represented power.

"I, too, have a gift for the child," said Amjad, and he handed Mary an ivory box. She cried out when she saw that the box was filled with frankincense. Frankincense was a rare spice that was burned in the temple in Jerusalem. It was a gift for a priest.

"I also have a gift for the child," Akash said as he handed Joseph a blue bottle. Joseph pulled the stopper from the bottle, and the scent of myrrh filled the room. Myrrh was an expensive oil that was used to anoint a king.

Our masters bowed toward Jesus and backed out the door. Joseph looked in the green bag and smelled the blue bottle. Mary ran her fingers through the frankincense in the ivory box.

Walking back to the caravan sites, Akash stated, "Tonight was special. I had dinner with people from many places, many classes, and many abilities, but I was comfortable with everyone. It was wonderful."

"Ah, the stories—that's what I'll remember: angels, dreams, miracles. It was as if we had a glimpse of God!" Amjad exclaimed.

"The people and the stories were wonderful, but I'll treasure the spirit in that room. Everyone was welcome. This king is like no other. I felt love tonight," Vaumisa observed.

We went to bed, but I didn't sleep. I paced back and forth, first in my tent and then outside. Vaumisa, Amjad, and Akash had decided to return to Jerusalem and tell Herod where Jesus was. Angels don't get anxious or worried, but we do get concerned. I was concerned about what Herod might do. God would protect Jesus, Mary, and Joseph, but what about my master, the widow, or even the people of Bethlehem? In just a few months we learned how evil Herod was. Trying to kill Jesus, he killed many baby boys in Bethlehem. So much pain, so much evil.

Vaumisa charged out of his tent and almost knocked me over. "Good, you're up, Felix," he said. "Everyone, get up. I want to be on our way before the sun comes up. Get packing."

"Where are we going, sir?" I asked.

"Home."

"By which route?" I asked.

"Not through Jerusalem. I had a dream to avoid Herod, but we need to leave soon," Vaumisa said. "I need to go tell my friends about my dream. Get everyone packing."

"Eloooree!" I shouted. Vaumisa gave me a questioning look and headed toward Amjad's camp.

Philos rushed in to our camp. "I bring a message from Akash!" Philos yelled. "We are leaving soon and will not go to Jerusalem. Akash had a dream giving him directions."

"So, did I," said Vaumisa. "Come with me to see Amjad." Vaumisa and Philos ran toward Amjad's camp. Amjad had also had a dream.

Soon the caravans were packed and ready to move out. Vaumisa, Amjad, and Akash said goodbye, and we headed away from Herod toward the Jordan River.

After we crossed the river, I said goodbye to Vaumisa, walked over the hill, did a triple somersault, yelled "Eloooree!" and flew back to heaven.

Egypt

When I arrived in heaven, I went to the Reflection Grotto to write my report. I wasn't taking any chances. I was doing missions again, and I wanted to keep doing them. When my report was finished, I thought about doing some proofreading but decided to wait. The commander hadn't told me to start proofreading again; I decided to say nothing until he said something. I dashed to Meditation Point where the SAAs were watching Earth.

"Soon they'll be in Egypt and will be safe," Philos said.

"Who's going to Egypt?" I asked.

"Jesus, Mary, and Joseph," Spero answered.

"Why?" I asked. Spero told me.

While we were sleeping outside Bethlehem, an angel appeared to Joseph and told him to leave Bethlehem and go to Egypt. Herod wanted to kill Jesus. While Mary packed, Joseph ran to the livestock market.

"Wake up! Wake up!" Joseph yelled as he pounded on the door.

"Shut up! You're upsetting the animals," the merchant growled as he opened the door. "What do you want?"

"I need a donkey," Joseph said.

"You need a donkey at this hour? The sun's not even up. Are you running from the authorities? I don't need any trouble."

"I need a donkey now. Would you sell me one for this gold coin?" Joseph asked as he pulled a gold coin from his robe.

The merchant looked at Joseph with his plain robe and worn sandals and then at the gold coin. "Who did you rob to get this coin? Don't tell me. I don't want to know. A gold coin for a donkey. Mmm, it's worth the risk," the merchant said. "Hurry, choose your donkey."

Joseph selected a donkey, handed the gold coin to the merchant, and led the donkey away.

"Forget where you got that donkey," the merchant said as he rubbed the gold on the sleeve of his robe.

Joseph hurried to the widow's house. Mary handed him two baskets containing Joseph's tools, their clothes, and a few other household items.

"I'm going to call this donkey Hosea," Mary said.

"I don't know about giving donkeys the names of prophets," Joseph said.

"Prophets have to be strong, just like donkeys," Mary replied. "Tie these baskets on Hosea."

Joseph shook his head and tied the baskets on Hosea. The widow stood watching with tears rolling down her cheeks. She gave Jesus a hug and kissed his curly black hair. Mary cried as she gave the widow a hug. "Here is a bowl I made; remember us," she said to the widow.

"I'll remember you always," the widow said. "What should I tell the kings when they come back?"

"I think they have already gone. Take these coins. They should take care of you for the rest of your life," Joseph said as he handed the widow several gold coins.

The widow stared at the coins. Never in her life had she held so much money. "Please don't go," she said as she tried to give Joseph the coins.

"We must. God told us to," Joseph said.

Joseph lifted Mary on to Hosea and gave her Jesus to hold. As the sun began to rise, they headed away from the tiny house on the narrow street to the highway leading to Egypt. By midday, they had joined a caravan heading south.

Gaudo, SAA, joined the caravan near Gaza. He had been sent to help Joseph and Mary. Joseph wouldn't speak to anyone. He was worried about Herod's spies. Sometimes, it's hard for SAAs to help people, especially if they are scared or worried.

SAAs cheered when the caravan crossed the border into Egypt. Gaudo approached Joseph. "There is a village close by, and I know the Jewish rabbi there. Would you like to meet him?" Gaudo asked.

"That would be helpful. Thank you," Joseph replied.

Egypt

With the help of the rabbi and Gaudo, Joseph was able to rent a house, join the local synagogue, and start his carpentry business. Mary made friends with the local women. Jesus played with the younger boys in the village. Mary gave birth to two more sons, James and Joses. The family had a nice life in Egypt, but they missed Nazareth. Mary especially worried about her mother. She prayed for her every day.

I was at Meditation Point when I felt a tingle. I pulled up a hologram of Jewish men at prayer in the Egyptian village synagogue. I did a couple of flips, yelled "Eloooree!" and sped toward Egypt. As I neared the village, I curled into a ball to slow my descent and took on the form of a young man as I landed near a market. I heard the chants of the Jewish men at prayer. I followed the sound until I found the synagogue. I pushed the door open and saw that Joseph was one of the men praying.

"Shalom, friend. Join us in prayer. What is your name, and where are you from?" the rabbi asked.

"My name is Felix. I am from a distant place but bring news from Jerusalem," I replied.

"What news?" Joseph asked.

"King Herod is dead."

The men nodded their heads and murmured, "Good news, good news."

"Maybe, maybe not. Archelaus is now king; he may be as bad as his father," I said.

"Let us pray for Israel and Jerusalem," the rabbi said. The men pulled their prayer shawls over their heads and prayed.

When we finished, Joseph invited me to dinner at his home. As we entered his yard, he called out, "Mary, King Herod is dead!"

Mary ran to the door holding a baby. "Oh, Joseph, do you think we can go home now?"

"Herod's son, Archelaus, is now king. He may be as dangerous as Herod."

"I really want to go home and see my mother," Mary said. "I want her to see our sons."

"I want to go home, too," Joseph said. "But we need to wait for God's direction."

Mary nodded, but I saw tears in her eyes. I quickly blinked and closed my eyes. I also felt tears. I couldn't let my angel identity slip out. I turned my head away and saw a green velvet bag, a blue bottle, and an ivory box sitting on a shelf. I remembered that wonderful night in Bethlehem.

"Felix, I need to straighten my carpentry shop. Would you like to see it?" Joseph asked.

"Yes, that would be nice," I said. I needed to get away from my memories. I started humming to myself.

"Come along, Jesus. You can help me," Joseph said. Jesus was sitting in a corner playing with a boy about four years old.

"Meet my sons," Joseph said. "Jesus is the oldest, then James is four, and the baby is Joses. God has been good to me."

Joseph showed me his carpentry shop. It was located in a shed near the front of his house. Saws, chisels, a mallet, a plum line, and a plane were hanging on the walls. A bow drill and a rule stick lay on his work bench.

"Jesus, stack the wood I used today while I oil my tools so they don't rust," Joseph said.

I picked up a small chisel and started carving a flower into a scrap piece of wood. I had never done that before. Apparently, I was going to need carpentry skills soon.

"That's amazing," Joseph said. "Are you a carpenter?"

"I have some skills," I said. "I'm trying to decide what to do, where to go."

"This is a nice village, but business can be slow. Right now, I'm making a storage chest for the rabbi. When that is finished, I have no more orders," Joseph said. "Jesus, come look at the olive blossom Felix has carved."

Jesus looked at my carving, nodded his head, and smiled.

"Dinner is ready when you are!" Mary called to us.

"Mary's a great cook; let's eat," Joseph said.

Jesus walked into the house and showed my carving to Mary. "How beautiful," she said. Jesus slipped my carved piece of wood into his pocket.

"Please excuse me," I said. "I just remembered something I must do." I ran out the door without looking back. Jesus, the Lord, the God of the Universe, wanted my little piece of wood. What an honor. I knew my angel identity would slip out. I dashed to a grove of palm trees, did a triple somersault, yelled Elooree! and sped back to heaven.

When I landed in heaven, the commander was waiting for me. "What are you doing here, Felix?

You did not finish your assignment in Egypt," he growled.

"I'm sorry, sir. I couldn't believe Jesus wanted that little flower I carved. I got so excited, I knew my angelic identity would come out," I said. "I just ran."

"I need to think about you and your problem. No more missions for you. While I'm thinking, you will go to Angel Bootcamp," the commander said as he walked away.

I spent several Earth months at Angel Bootcamp. I was practicing my calming breath—breathe in slowly, hold, breathe out very slowly—when the commander approached. "Felix, after much discussion in the Angelic Council, we have decided to give you another chance. I'm sending you back to complete your mission."

I jumped up and spun around. "Thank you, sir! Thank you, sir!" I yelled. "Thank you for giving me another chance. You won't regret it."

"Go, Felix, go. Joseph needs you," the commander said, shaking his head.

I glanced at the home of Joseph and Mary. The sun was just coming up.

Mary reached over to wake Joseph, but he wasn't there. "Joseph, where are you?" she called as she shook Jesus awake.

Joseph came into the room with a plate of bread and honey.

"What's so special that we can have honey?" Mary asked.

He smiled at Mary and said, "It's time to go home. An angel came to me in a dream last night. It's safe to return to Israel."

"Really, Joseph? We can go home?" Mary smiled as she dipped bread into the honey and handed it to Jesus and James.

"I have some jobs I must finish, and then we can go home." Joseph replied. "You decide what you want to take with you and give the rest away." Joseph took a bit of bread dipped in honey and walk out the door to his shop.

Triple flip, Eloooree! Egypt, here I come.

I landed outside the village and headed to Joseph's house. "Shalom, Joseph, How's business?" I asked when I reached his shop.

"Well, look who it is! Felix, what happened to you several months ago? You didn't just leave our house; you disappeared completely," Joseph said.

"I'm sorry for how I acted. You were so nice to me," I replied. "I just needed to be by myself for a while."

"Are you okay now?" Joseph asked. "What are you doing here?"

"I'm fine, and I'm just passing through. I wondered if you could use an assistant for a few days," I replied.

"I could. We're going back to Israel, but I must finish two doors, a bench, and a plow before we can leave," Joseph said. "Help me get the work done in three weeks, and I will pay you one gold coin."

"Deal."

I was doing much better; my angel identity didn't slip out at all. Breathe in, hold, breathe out slowly.

While we worked, Mary sorted through their furnishings. She had things piled all around the house. One day, Joseph looked at the piles and asked, "Mary, which of these piles go with us?"

"Don't worry, Joseph. I plan for Amos, our new donkey, to carry Jesus and James, our clothes, a few rugs, and some food, and we can carry your tools in this basket. We must give away our furniture and our pottery. Is that okay?"

"I wonder if I should leave my tools; they're heavy. I left my old tools with your mother. What do you think, Mary?" Joseph asked.

"Joseph, how will you provide for us without your tools? I think we should take them. We don't know what we will find in Nazareth. Will our house still be there? Will our furniture be there?" Mary answered.

I was working in the shop and heard Mary and Joseph. "I'll make bigger baskets that you can tie on Amos. Amos can carry the tools, not you," I offered.

Several days later, Joseph, Mary, Jesus, James, and Joses were part of a caravan heading to Israel. Jesus and James sat on a pile of rugs on the back of Amos. Behind them I tied two large baskets. One held Joseph's tools, and the other held food for the trip and a green velvet bag, a blue bottle, and an ivory box. Everyone wore the clothes they were taking to Nazareth. I slipped my gold coin into Mary's pocket. SAAs have no need for money.

Mary carried Joses as she walked, skipped, and even ran next to the donkey. Joseph carried a few pots on his back so that he could draw water from wells as they traveled.

"You have been a big help, Felix. Thanks," Joseph said as he shook my hand.

"There's not much carpentry work in the village. Do you mind if I walk with you? Maybe I can find some work along the way," I replied.

"Anyone can walk these roads, and I'll be glad to have the company. We'll be glad to share our food with you," Joseph replied. "Would you carry one of these pots?"

I took the biggest pot off Joseph's back and started my trip to Nazareth. Along the way, I taught Joseph how to carve decorations in wood with a chisel.

Nazareth

As we entered the hill country of Judea, Mary showed Jesus and James the birds and the flowers. I wondered if she remembered that Jesus had created the birds, the flowers, the rocks, the streams—everything. James laughed when a small yellow bird landed on Jesus' finger. Jesus showed James how to gently stroke the bird. The bird tweeted a concert for us. Jesus held his hand up and the bird flew away. James held out his finger, but no bird came to him.

We went around a curve and saw Nazareth in the distance. Mary ran ahead and called out, "The house is still there!"

"And the door is gone. That's not a good sign," Joseph said when he, the boys, and Amos caught up with her. "Let's go see what's inside."

The house was there, but it needed a new roof. The furniture was gone. The olive tree and the fig tree were still there, but the garden was filled with weeds.

While Joseph spread rugs over the holes in the roof and cleared a rat's nest from the house, Mary went to see her mother. I went along to help bring back her wedding chest and Joseph's tools. Mary knocked on the door of Anne's house. Miriam opened the door.

"Miriam, what are you doing here? Where is my mother?" Mary asked, looking around.

"Oh, Mary. Anne died. I'm so sorry. Anne moved to her family home in Cana when you didn't return from Bethlehem," Miriam explained. "About four years ago, Anne sold her house to Eli. I married him a couple of months later. Mary, where have you been?"

"Oh, it's a very long story; I'll tell you someday. When did my mother die?" Mary asked.

"I guess she must have died about two years ago," Miriam replied. "She left your wedding chest for you and Joseph's tools. Let me get them."

Joseph was delighted when Mary and I returned, carrying his tools and the wedding chest, until he saw Mary's red eyes. "What's the matter, Mary?"

"My mother is dead. She died two years ago. She never met Jesus, James, or Joses," Mary sobbed.

Joseph wiped his eyes. "Oh, Mary, Nazareth won't be the same without her. She was so good to you when I didn't believe you. I always thank God for Anne. Is there anything I can do for you?"

Reaching out to Joseph, Mary said, "Hold me for a minute. Then we must get to work repairing and cleaning the house. My mother always quoted the proverb: *"If you work hard, you will have plenty. If you do nothing but talk, you will not have enough."* [3]

"Could you use my help in fixing up the house?" I asked Joseph the next morning. "I'm willing to work for food and a place to sleep."

Joseph chuckled and said, "I can offer you another gold coin for your help, or maybe you would prefer frankincense or myrrh."

"Joseph, I didn't know you were the high priest or the governor. Such riches," I said. "No, a roof over my head and food in my stomach are enough."

Joseph shook his head and said, "Deal."

Jesus helped us gather the branches needed for a new roof. We added a new layer of branches, rolled them flat, and then added a new layer of clay. Joseph made a new door, Jesus oiled it, and I hung it. Joseph and I made a new table and bench while Mary made a few clay pots. Jesus and I helped Mary weed the garden and stake the grape vines. Mary, Jesus, and I took turns watching James and Joses.

Soon we had the house in good shape, and Mary and Joseph and their children went to Cana. Mary wanted to talk to her uncles. I said goodbye and walked away from Nazareth. Once outside town, I yelled Eloooree! did a triple somersault, and flew back to heaven.

The commander met me when I arrived in heaven. "This mission had a rough start but a good ending."

"Thank you, sir. I think," I replied.

"You let your angelic identity slip out and left a mission without finishing it. SAAs always finish their missions. You went back, worked close to Jesus, and kept calm and under control. Continue to practice your breathing, your focusing exercises, and your humming. I need you on Earth; you are good with people." The commander said and walked away.

"Eloooree," I whispered.

Jerusalem

There are three major festivals in the Jewish religion, and Jews tried to be in Jerusalem for the celebrations. Joseph and Mary enjoyed the festivals and seeing Zechariah and Elizabeth. Both families camped outside Jerusalem. John and Jesus entertained the other children in the campsite including Jesus' half brothers—James, Joses, Simon, and Jude—and his half sisters. In the mornings, John and Jesus played games with the children: races, tag, and hide-and-go-seek. In the afternoons when it was hot, Jesus told stories about God to the children. Once they acted out the parting of the Red Sea. Jesus led the children down a path (the Red Sea). Then they went on a walk to a small hill where everyone recited the Ten Commandments. It was amazing to see the author of the Ten Commandments repeating them with a group of little children.

Jews were celebrating Passover, the most important of the festivals. SAAs were busy everywhere in Israel, helping people get to Jerusalem for the celebration. We did everything and anything. We gave directions, shared food, carried children, helped set up camps, mended broken carts, chased runaway donkeys, and bandaged cuts and bruises. You name it, we did it. I didn't think I could get an assignment I hadn't done, but I did.

When Philos and I finished setting up a camp for a family from Hebron, we headed over the hill to go back to heaven. I felt a tingle and opened a hologram of me stacking wood in a cave. I was tired and wanted to go back to heaven.

"Philos, let's start gathering wood," I said.

"Why?" Philos asked.

"Didn't you get the new orders to stack wood in a cave?"

"No, I'm on my way back to heaven," Philos replied.

"Wait, I get to gather wood and you get to go to heaven. I wonder who I upset," I replied. "And I thought I was doing well."

"Enjoy," Philos said as he did a triple flip, yelled Eloooree! and disappeared into the cosmos.

I found a shallow cave near the olive groves outside Jerusalem. Gather wood, stack in cave, gather wood, stack in cave, over and over again. Thunder rumbled in the distance, and I felt a plop of rain on my hand, then another and another. Soon rain was pouring down. Every step I took was SQUISH, SPLAT, SQUISH, SPLAT. I was slipping and sliding and covered in mud. Finally, the rain stopped. Why had I gathered all that wood? It seemed pointless.

I walked out of the woods into a campsite. Mary was standing in the middle of a campsite, wringing out her robe and kicking the remains of a fire with her wet sandal. "Elizabeth, what are we going to do? We need to cook the lamb for Passover, but all the wood is wet."

Now I knew why I had gathered all that wood.

"Shalom, if you will give me your wet wood, I will bring you dry wood," I said to Mary.

Mary stepped back, pushed her wet hair under her scarf, and stared at me.

"I have dry wood," I said. "Just give me your wet wood, and I'll bring you dry wood."

"Why would you do that?" she asked. "Everyone in these olive groves needs dry wood. You could sell it."

"Call me a fool. I have dry wood, and I'll give it to you," I replied. "Just give me your wet wood."

"Take the wet wood. I can't cook over it," Mary said.

Off I went with the wet wood and stored it in the cave. I gathered logs, twigs, and hay and hurried back to Mary's campsite. I stacked twigs in the firepit, placed hay in a notch in my fireboard, and spun a small branch in the notch until the hay caught fire. I tossed the burning hay onto the twigs. When the twigs caught fire, I added logs. Mary had fire for cooking.

When others noticed I had started a fire for Mary, they asked me to start fires for them. Run, stack, whirl, CRACKLE, toss! Run, stack, whirl, CRACKLE, toss! Run, stack, whirl, CRACKLE, toss! Soon, the hills outside Jerusalem were dotted with cook fires.

Mary invited me to stay for dinner, and I gladly accepted.

After dinner, Mary said to Zechariah, "Our sons are special."

"Everyone feels that way about their sons," Zechariah replied.

"Yes, but you know what I mean. They're miracles," Mary said. "Please write down the story of John's birth."

"I'd love to. I'll bring writing materials the next time we meet. Then, I'll write down the story of Jesus' birth," Zechariah answered. "Joseph, I will need details from you to make the story complete. Do we have a deal?"

"Of course, we do. I'll make a special box. I'll decorate it with carved olive blossoms for Israel, palm leaves for Egypt, and a star on top. I'll make it big enough to hold John's story, Jesus' story, Mary's song, the blue bottle, the ivory box, and the green velvet bag. Mary, please sing that song now," Joseph replied.

Mary started to sing, "I praise the Lord with all my heart. I am very happy because God is my Savior." Soon, the hillside filled with praises to God.

I fell asleep listening to Mary. Just before sunrise, I woke up. I should have gone back to heaven as soon as my job was finished. I heard the call for morning prayer. I decided to take a chance. I asked for permission to go to the Passover celebration before I went back to heaven. Much to my surprise, the commander said, "Yes, if you provide wood for the campfires tonight."

I checked the cave, and the wet wood was dry. I celebrated all morning and then returned to the campsites. I asked Mary if she needed wood for the meal that night.

"Of course, I do. Jesus and John, help gather the wood for cooking."

I couldn't believe it; I was working directly with Jesus and John. Soon, we had given dry wood to many campsites. I was about to leave when Mary asked me to eat the Passover meal with them. "We have a Passover meal because of your wood."

I celebrated the Passover feast with Joseph and Zechariah and their families. We ate bread made without yeast, bitter herbs, fruit and honey, eggs, and lamb. As we ate, the families asked the boys what they had learned at the temple that day.

"Father, I will soon be a man; what does God want from me?" thirteen-year-old John asked.

"John, when I was your age, I thought God wanted me to do everything perfectly, but that's impossible," Zechariah said. "God wants us to love him and each other. If you come to God with a grateful and willing spirit, he will tell what he wants from you."

"That's much harder than obeying a list of rules," John answered.

"Yes, it is, John. Trust in the Lord, and all will be fine," Zechariah replied. "It is late, boys. Go to bed; we must start for home tomorrow."

I headed home to heaven that night. Elooooree! flip, flip, flip, zoom.

When I got to heaven, I watched a special campsite.

The next day, the families said goodbye. Joseph and his family joined others from Nazareth for the long walk home. When the travelers stopped for the night, Joseph went to get Jesus to help set up camp.

"Mary, where is Jesus?" he asked. "I need his help."

Mary spun around and replied, "I thought he was with you."

"No, he was with you, wasn't he?" Joseph answered.

Without even replying, Mary hurried off to the other women and children, but no one had seen

Jesus. The men began to search the campsite, but no one could remember seeing Jesus on the road.

Joseph, Mary, and their other children hurried back to Jerusalem. They looked in the market and the campsite, but they couldn't find Jesus. Joseph remembered that Jesus enjoyed listening to the rabbis. The family ran to the temple. How would they find Jesus in the vast temple complex?

They asked everyone if they had seen a twelve-year-old boy wearing a brown robe. Yes, they had seen many twelve-year-old boys, and most of them were wearing brown robes. I saw Spero among the temple crowd. He said to Joseph, "I think you'll find the boy in that group of men."

Joseph and Mary hurried over and heard Jesus before they saw him. Joseph pushed his way through the crowd. Jesus was talking with the religious teachers. In a stern voice, Joseph said, "Jesus, why didn't you come with us when we left Jerusalem?"

Mary continued, "Your father and I were very worried about you. We have been looking everywhere for you."

Jesus replied, *"Why did you have to look for me? You should have known that I must be where my Father's work is."* [4]

Everyone looked at Joseph, and he stepped back into the crowd. I heard teachers whispering, "His father's work? Doesn't he come from Nazareth? Isn't his father a carpenter?"

Mary stepped forward and said, "That is true, but now you must come home with us."

Jesus nodded, stood up, and stepped toward Mary. Several teachers reached out to stop him, but Jesus shook his head no. Jesus led Mary, Joseph, and his brothers and sisters out of the temple.

I didn't realize how different the next Passovers would be. Zechariah and Elizabeth died, and John went to live in the desert. Several years later, Joseph died, and Jesus became the head of the family.

Nazareth

Jesus lived like his neighbors. He worked hard as a carpenter. He rejoiced at births and weddings and mourned at funerals. As the head of the family, he found wives for his brothers and husbands for his sisters. He took care of his mother. SAAs weren't sent to Nazareth often; Jesus didn't need our help. We did watch what happened there.

Jesus taught his brothers to be carpenters. They worked under the olive tree in the courtyard of Joseph's house (now Jesus' house). Jesus, the creator of the Universe, was an excellent carpenter. People ordered tables, doors, benches, roof beams, and even plows and yokes for oxen. Jesus would carve bowls or spoons if needed.

When women came to visit Mary, they brought their children. The children and Jesus played. Jesus had a box of wooden animals he had carved for the children. It was amazing to watch Jesus tell the story of Noah's ark using his carved animals. When the sun was hot, Jesus sat under the olive tree and told stories from the Old Testament. Once he marched around the courtyard as Joshua, and all the children followed him. Thankfully, the walls didn't come tumbling down when he made the "ta-doo, ta-doo" sound of a trumpet.

Every year just before the trip to Jerusalem for Passover, Mary would pull out Joseph's box. Her fingers caressed the olive branches and palm leaves carved in the sides and the star on the top. She read the stories by Joseph and Zechariah and sang her song. She smelled the myrrh and frankincense and felt the gold coins. She rubbed the olive blossom I had carved and Jesus had added to the box. The box was taken to Jerusalem each year for Passover. A tradition was developed that the boy closest to twelve years of age had to carry the box. Mary could not explain why she wanted the box with her; she just knew she wanted it.

Life was going well in Nazareth, and no one could see any reason for it to change—no one but Mary and Jesus.

I was finishing up a mission in Joppa when I felt the jolt of an All SAA Command. Everyone returned to SAA Headquarters where we learned that John, Jesus' cousin, would soon be preaching in the Jordan Valley. We were to travel throughout Galilee and Judah and encourage people to go hear John. My assignment was Galilee, especially the towns of Cana, Rumah, and Nazareth. I was also to stop at any markets or villages along my route.

I had been on the road for a month when I arrived in Nazareth, my final stop. I set up my stall as a seller of tools. I told everyone who came to my stall about John the Baptist.

Jesus and his brother, James, walked toward me. I hadn't been near Jesus in a long time. Would I be able to handle it? My knees started to bend. *No,* I told myself. *Keep your angel in.* SAAs had strict orders not to worship Jesus while he was on Earth. Breathe, hum; breathe, hum. He's getting closer. Breathe, hum. He's here. "Shalom, and how may I help you?" I did it.

"I need some nails and maybe a new awl," James answered. "Where are you from, and do you have any news?"

I got out some nails and a selection of awls. "I'm from the Jordan River Valley, and something wonderful is happening there. There is a new prophet named John the Baptist. He is urging people to repent."

"Tell us about this John," James said. "Where's he from? Who are his parents? Who did he study with?"

"His parents were Zechariah and Elizabeth, but they died many years ago," I said. "When his parents died, he moved to the wilderness and studied with religious groups."

"Jesus, do you realize that this is our relative? Mother will be glad to know about John," James replied. "Please tell us about John. How is he doing?"

"He's a preacher, and many call him a prophet."

"So, he's a religious leader?" James asked.

"Not the type you're thinking of. No fancy robes for him; he wears clothing made of camel's hair with a leather belt. No rich food either; he eats locusts and wild honey," I replied. "He has made quite an impression; many come out from Jerusalem to see and hear him."

"Really, who comes to see him?" James asked.

"Everybody and anybody—ordinary people, tax collectors, soldiers, even religious leaders."

"What does John say?" James asked.

"Repent and be baptized," I replied.

"Do the people obey him?"

"Yes, many people are baptized every day. Only God knows if they have repented," I answered. "Not everyone is happy with John. The political and religious leaders are nervous about the large crowds."

"Thank you for the information," James said as he handed me several coins to pay for their nails. "Jesus, let's go tell Mother about John; she will be so pleased." Jesus and James hurried away from the market.

Now, you must understand that none of this information was news to Jesus. Since he is God, he knows all. Jesus doesn't need our help, but people need to be directed to Jesus.

I spent the day telling people about John the Baptist. A young boy sat on the ground next to my stall. He tried to sell small bowls and lamps without success. At the end of the day, I gave him my stall, slipped my money into one of his bowls, and walked down the road that ran in front of Jesus' house. I heard James replying to something Jesus had said.

"I understand that you want to go see John, but what do you mean you must be about your father's business? Your father's business was carpentry. So is your business and mine!" James yelled. "Of course, I'll take care of Mother and keep watch over our brothers and sisters and the business, but you are such a good carpenter; we need you."

Jesus smiled and walked inside the house.

James called out to him, "You tell Mother your news! She'll be upset. Tell the rest of the family at dinner tonight. I want them to know it's your idea to go to the Jordan River."

I walked down the road wondering what would happen next. Flip, flip, flip, Eloooree, and away.

Jordan River

I was entering my report into the database when I felt a tingle and opened a hologram of a teenage girl playing a harp for a wealthy older woman. Was I the woman or the girl? Only one way to find out. I leapt into the cosmos with a shout of Eloooree!

Arriving as a teenage girl holding a small harp, I walked down the streets of Jerusalem while I pondered how to find my assignment.

"Hey, you girl with the harp!" a man shouted at me.

"Yes, sir," I replied.

"Can you play that harp?" he asked.

"Yes, sir," I replied and began to play the accompaniment to Psalm 67 and sing:

> God, show mercy to us and bless us.
> Please accept us!
> Let everyone on earth learn about you.
> Let every nation see how you save people.

"Enough, you'll do," the man said. "You look like you could use a job. Am I right?"

"Yes, sir. Who are you?" I said as I looked at my ragged dress and worn sandals.

"I am Ehud, the manager of the house of Malon. You will be the companion and maid to his mother. If you want the job, quit asking questions and come with me," Ehud replied and started walking away.

If Malon had a manager, he was probably wealthy, and his mother would be elderly. This woman could be my mission. I hurried after Ehud. We entered a large house and he said, "Put on these clothes, and I'll introduce you to your new mistress."

I slipped a dark green robe over my tattered dress, tied sturdy brown sandals on my feet, and wrapped my hair in a tan scarf. I picked up my harp and followed Ehud into a large room where an elegant lady sat at a desk writing a letter and sipping from a cup.

"Ehud, send this letter by runner to Joanna, wife of Chuza. You know he is the manager of King Herod's property and is a very wealthy man. She is wealthy, too. I thought she would like to go shopping in the markets of Jerusalem. She is staying in Jericho at her brother's house, the house with the blue door. I am inviting her to come and stay with us for several weeks."

"Mistress Susanna, your son Malon has given orders that you should go to the country house near the Jordan River and stay there until he calls you home. You will leave tomorrow morning," Ehud stated.

"No!" Susanna screamed as she threw her cup at us. Wine splashed everywhere; Ehud ducked, and I knelt down to pick up the cup.

"I will not go!" Susanna shouted. "This is the doing of his new wife, Abigail. Who does she think she is? I am from an important family in Jerusalem. My husband was the wealthiest grain merchant in Israel. Our family provides wheat for the grain offering at the temple. Abigail is from Bethlehem, and her father was a shepherd. I want to speak to Malon."

"Malon left this morning to go to Caesarea. He is to sign a contract to supply grain to the Romans," Ehud replied as he stepped back and pushed me forward. "I have hired Felicia to be your companion and maid while you are in the countryside. She plays the harp. Play for us." Ehud gave me a push toward Susanna and left the room. I started to strum my harp and singing Psalm 103:

> My soul, praise the Lord!
> Every part of me, praise his holy name!
> My soul, praise the Lord
> and never forget how kind he is!

"Oh, shut up!" Susanna yelled at me. "I must think."

She filled a cup with wine and left the room. "Come, girl; you have work to do."

After a period of screaming and crying, Susanna decided to go to the country house and invite Joanna to join her there. She wrote another letter and sent it by runner to Jericho.

It was a long evening as Susanna yelled at everyone, complained about everything, and drank cup after cup of wine. Finally, she passed out. With help from Ehud and several other servants, we packed Susanna's clothes, jewelry, and wine and loaded them on a horse-drawn cart. At dawn, we headed to the country house.

After a long and difficult journey, we arrived at the country house. There was good news: Joanna was coming. In fact, she would be here in just a couple of days.

The country house servants and I scrubbed, swept, and polished so that the house would be ready for company. I felt that we had to do everything twice, because nothing was good enough for our mistress. The creak of wagon wheels outside the house was a joyful sound. Susanna snapped at me to open the door. Joanna climbed out of a horse-drawn carriage, and for the first time I saw Susanna smile.

These two women had grown up together, but they were nothing alike. When I played a song on the harp, Joanna wanted to hear psalms; Susanna wanted to hear Roman drinking songs. If I told a story, Joanna wanted to hear something from the Bible; Susanna wanted to hear stories of the Greek gods. When we went for a walk, Joanna admired the flowers; Susanna complained about the heat. Once we came across a family walking toward the Jordan River. Joanna asked them where they were going. "We're going to hear the new preacher, John the Baptist. They say he is different from the priests."

That evening while I was playing music, Joanna said, "Why don't we take a trip to the Jordan and find this new preacher? People everywhere are talking about him. It will be a change for us."

"You want to go hear a preacher?" Susanna asked. "You are bored, but so am I. Yes, let's go. It will better than looking at flowers or listening to Felicia."

The next morning, our small caravan set out. Susanna insisted on bringing food, tents, chairs, rugs, bedding, and her wine. Soon we saw a crowd waiting for the preacher. The servants set up an awning and two chairs for our mistresses. Susanna drank wine, Joanna ate grapes, and I sat on the ground behind them and played my harp.

A wild-looking man walked over a hill on the opposite bank of the river. "Repent, for the kingdom of heaven is near, and be baptized to show that you have repented!" John yelled.

The crowd began to move. Someone jostled the awning; another bumped Susanna's chair. "Watch out! Keep your distance!" she yelled. "Don't you know who I am?"

The crowd kept moving, and many entered the water to be baptized.

The religious leaders from Jerusalem watched John from a hill. John pointed at them and said, "You brood of vipers! Who warned you to listen to me? You must repent."

Susanna stood up and shouted, "How dare you speak to the temple leaders that way?" She then turned to Joanna. "Let's go back to the tent. I've had enough of this wild man," she grumbled as she walked up the hill drinking her wine. Joanna rose from her seat and started up the hill. I followed, dragging both chairs, the awning, and my harp.

We settled down early that evening. Susanna fell asleep while eating dinner, and Joanna sat in the corner thinking. The next morning, Susanna said we should go home, but Joanna wanted to stay one more day. Joanna was a guest, so Susanna agreed. I lugged everything down to the riverside again.

John appeared early and waded straight into the river. He started to preach, and people came forward to be baptized. About noon, the crowd parted, and I saw Jesus walking toward the river. He stepped into the water and walked toward John.

John stood there shaking his head no. "I should be baptized by you," John said to Jesus.

"Let it be this way for now. We should do whatever God says is right," Jesus answered. [5]

John stepped forward and baptized Jesus. As Jesus came out of the water, a dove landed on him and a voice from heaven said, *"This is my Son, the one I love. I am very pleased with him."* [6]

Jesus walked out of the water on the other side and over the hill. John left the river and did not return that day. The crowds went home.

"That was incredible!" Joanna said. "Who was that? Where did the voice come from? Who was speaking? Did you see the dove land on him? The dove didn't fear him at all."

"They call him Jesus," I answered. "The voice was the voice of God, and the dove represented the Spirit of God."

"Be quiet, Felicia. You, silly girl, you are not a priest, a temple assistant, or a rabbi. You're talking about things you know nothing about," Susanna said.

"Susanna, I think Felicia is right. Something very special happened in front of us. We have been blessed. I'm going for a walk so I can think," Joanna said.

At dinner that night, Joanna asked, "What did John mean by 'Repent, for the kingdom of God is coming'? Do you think he meant that the Savior, the Messiah, is coming? Maybe John is the Savior."

"Joanna, do you really believe in a Savior or Messiah?" Susanna asked.

"Yes, I do," Joanna answered. "What about you, Felicia?"

"Why are you asking her?" Susanna said.

"I think she knows more than us about this subject," Joanna answered. "What do you think, Felicia?"

"I do believe in a Savior, but I don't think it is John. It is Jesus," I replied.

"Who's Jesus?" Susanna asked.

"The man that John baptized, the heavenly voice spoke about, and the dove landed on," I replied.

Soon we went to bed. Joanna and Susanna slept inside the tent. The servants, including me, slept on the ground outside. About midnight, I heard someone crying. I got up to investigate. It was Susanna.

"Mistress, what's the matter? What can I do for you?" I asked.

"How do I repent? What does 'repent' mean?" she asked.

"It means to change. Everyone has different things they need to change. You cannot change on your own; you need God's help. To repent means to ask God to change you," I explained.

"Do you think God will listen to me? I haven't worshipped him in a long time. I just go to the services."

"If you really seek him, you will find him," I answered.

"I have been unhappy for a long time. I want to change. Get me up early tomorrow, so I can listen to John again."

"Yes, ma'am."

Susanna went back into the tent. I lay down, but I didn't sleep. As soon as the sun started to rise, I woke both Susanna and Joanna.

Soon we were heading for the river. Susanna was scanning the far bank for John. When he appeared, she walked into the water and spoke with John. As John baptized Susanna, I heard Joanna gasp. Then she headed into the water. Those two dripping wet women sat on the grass all day listening to John.

That night they decided to go home, but not before Susanna had mapped out a course of study, prayer, and meditation for them to use when they got home. I spent the next thirty days with Susanna and Joanna, helping them to understand God's love and his ways.

A letter arrived for Joanna. She was invited to a wedding in Cana in Galilee.

"Susanna, come with me to Cana and then on to my house. We can continue our studies."

"I think I will, Joanna," Susanna replied. "When should we leave?"

"The sooner, the better," Joanna answered.

"Felicia, come here," Susanna called. "We're going to Cana in Galilee and then on to Joanna's house. We need to start planning and packing,"

"Mistress, please release me from my job. I need to return to my home. There are things I need to do," I replied. I had been called back to heaven, but I didn't want to disappear. Susanna was changing, but she still needed help.

"This is a shock, Felicia. How will I get along without you?" Susanna said.

"I'll find a maid for you before I leave, and we'll have you packed and ready to go. I know a girl in the village I think would be very good," I replied.

"Bring her to meet me tomorrow. Please don't go. I depend on you,"

"I'll have her here at midday tomorrow. Her name is Yael. She also plays the harp, and her father is a rabbi, so she knows scripture."

Susanna liked Yael, and about a week later, I left. I walked over the hill, yelled Eloooree! and leapt into the cosmos and back to heaven. When I landed, the commander was waiting for me. *I know I haven't done anything wrong,* I thought.

"Welcome back, Felix," the commander said. "Congratulations on a job well done. I have a hologram of worship at the Crystal Sea the day Susanna was baptized. Take a look."

The angels were singing praises to God when the silver trumpets blew. A herald angel stepped forward and proclaimed, "Susanna, mother of Malon, has turned from her wicked ways. Praise and glory to God for his mercy and grace." All the angels cheered and cheered. I flipped and yelled Eloooree! It's so good when someone returns to God. Praise be to God.

I walked away, remembering my time by the Jordan River. I remembered the baptism of Jesus. I wondered what Jesus was going to do now. His time as a carpenter in Nazareth was finished. Would he go to Jerusalem as a prophet like Isaiah or Jeremiah? Would he lead an army like David or Joshua? He didn't do any of these things. He did something I never expected.

Judean Wilderness

I was finishing a report on a mission in Jericho when Lt. Parebo walked up. "Felix, take a look toward the wilderness where Jesus has been fasting and praying," he said.

"I can't believe that Jesus, the Lord of the Universe, needed to fast and pray," I replied.

"We don't understand his mission, but we know he always does the right thing," Lt. Parebo answered.

I glanced at Earth and saw a dark shadow falling across the rough and rugged wilderness. "Is that who I think it is?" I asked.

"Yes, it's Satan. He's coming to tempt Jesus."

"It'll never work," I said.

"The SAAs are at Meditation Point to watch this fight. Let's go. It should be good," Lt Parebo said.

We headed to Meditation Point where any SAAs who weren't on a mission had gathered. We had a long history with Satan and wanted to see him defeated.

Satan is an angel, an archangel like Michael. Or he was until he was thrown out of heaven for rebelling against God. Many think Satan has horns and a tail, and sometimes he does. At other times, he's attractive and smart. Sometimes he's ugly and scary. Satan can be hard to recognize, and he'll try to trick you.

Satan has many ways to trick people into following him. He knows you have physical needs, and he'll use those needs to tempt you.

Jesus was resting in a valley in the wilderness. He sat on a large rock when a plump man came down the path eating bread. Snakes slithered out and curled up to block the path.

"Do you slimy creatures think you can stop me?" Satan said. "Go back under your rocks where you belong."

Satan stepped over the snakes and smiled at Jesus. Popping the last piece of bread in his mouth, Satan said, "You look hungry, very hungry. I was a bad boy; I ate all the bread. Too bad."

Satan walked around looking at the rocks. "I have an idea. You can change stones into bread. This would be a simple miracle for you. Here is a big rock; it would give you bread for several days. Turn these little rocks into bread, and you could have a snack whenever you wanted. You don't need my bread; you can make your own. No more hunger. Come on Jesus, turn rocks into bread. You can do it. You know you can. Do it now. What are you waiting for?"

Jesus turned his head and answered Satan with scripture. He said, *"A person does not live only by eating bread."* [7]

"Fool!" Satan said as he glared at Jesus and walked away, almost stepping on the snakes who hissed at him until he was out of sight.

The SAAs clapped and cheered.

Jesus used scripture to answer Satan, but Satan knows scripture and will use it to confuse people.

After a bit, Satan came down the path as a gladiator. Wolves jumped into the path to block Satan. "Do you think I'm frightened by your snarling teeth?" Satan sneered. "Go back in your caves," he ordered as he pulled a knife from his belt and slashed at the wolves.

"Jesus, I've come to help you. As a gladiator, I know about putting on a show. Come with me to Jerusalem. I have an idea for how to get your ministry off to an amazing start. Stand on the top of the temple. My assistants will blow trumpets to get everyone's attention. Jump from the top of the temple. God has promised in the Psalms that angels will hold you up, and you won't even hurt your foot. After the angels put you down, you can preach and teach. The crowds will be enormous. The governor will want to hear you; the emperor may ask to see you. All you have to do is trust God to keep his promise. Do you trust him? If you trust God, come with me to Jerusalem. Right now, no time to wait, let's get this show on the road."

Jesus shook his head and said, *"You must not test the Lord your God."* [8]

Satan shrieked and ran down the path, pushing the wolves out of his way. The wolves chased Satan until he disappeared.

The SAAs yelled Eloooree! I wondered if the demons were watching this battle. If so, they weren't having as much fun as we were.

Satan is known as the father of lies, so he approves of cheating, stealing, and fighting. He tried to get Jesus to cheat.

The sound of trumpets echoed off the valley walls. Six trumpeters, followed by a king dressed in red and purple with jeweled rings on his fingers and a gold crown on his head, came down the path. A lion jumped down to block the path. "Out of my way, silly kitty!" Satan roared. "Do you think you can scare me? Away; go take a cat nap." Satan shoved the lion away.

"Jesus, as you know, I am king of this world. I know that you want to save this world. How do you plan to do that? Your plan probably involves sacrifice and pain. I have a better plan. If you do what I ask, you will win all the continents and all the people on this little planet; it's not worth suffering for. I'm not asking much for this world. All you need to do, Jesus, is kneel before me and say, 'Satan is the greatest' and 'I love Satan.'"

Before Satan could even encourage Jesus to obey him, Jesus stood up and shouted, *"Get away from me, Satan!"* [9] and then he said, *"Respect the Lord your God and serve only him."* [10]

Satan howled, tore his robe, tossed his rings to the ground, and threw his crown at the lion. He raised his hands and disappeared into a column of red smoke. I heard him yell as he disappeared, "I'll be back!"

Angels descended to Earth. They brought bread and water to Jesus. When he was refreshed, he walked out of the wilderness and headed north to Galilee.

The SAAs cheered, flipped, and leaped. Jesus had defeated Satan. Then Lt. Parebo said, "Great victory, but Satan promised to return, and that's a promise he'll keep. He will also try to trick your people, so be on your guard."

Cana

I was in the Majestic Forest practicing my focusing exercises when I felt a tingle. The hologram showed a wedding feast. I love parties, but I wondered what my mission was. The wedding was in Cana, and the groom was a relative of Mary. Maybe I would see Mary or Jesus.

A day before the wedding, I landed near Cana as a teenage boy. As I walked into town, Mary hired me to serve at the wedding. She was in charge of the food and drink and needed more servers. What a delight to be working with Mary!

Serving at a wedding is not as easy as it looks. Six large water jars lined the path to the garden. Guests would wash their hands with the water in these jars when they arrived. Several servants, including me, had to fill these jars. We carried large buckets of water from the well at the back of the garden to the jars at the front, over and over and over again. As I was stretching my back, Mary called to me and two others.

"You seem like responsible young men. You will be in charge of serving the wine. Tomorrow morning, wash the cups and fill pitchers with wine from the supply near the kitchen. Then, decorate the wine table with grapes and flowers."

"Yes, ma'am," we replied.

The next day started early. This was a large wedding, and we washed over a hundred cups. My fellow servants started throwing soapy water around. By the time we washed and rinsed the cups several times, soapy water was everywhere. We were drenched and running late. We filled the nine large pitchers with wine and arranged the cups on trays before the guests arrived. The table was not decorated. The other wine servers took trays of cups filled with wine to the guests while I arranged grapes and flowers.

Mary dashed through the garden saying, "He's here! He's here!"

I looked toward the entrance to the garden and saw Jesus hugging his mother. Jesus had come and brought several friends. Soon Jesus' brothers arrived with their families. It was quite a family reunion. The men discussed business and the news of Israel. James told Jesus that the carpentry business was doing well, but they could use his help. Joses told anyone who would listen about his newborn son. Simon talked to some fishermen about building fishing boats. Everyone was having a wonderful time.

I tilted a pitcher to pour more wine, but it was empty; every pitcher was empty. The wine jars by the kitchen were empty. "Ma'am, where can I get more wine?" I asked Mary.

Mary hurried over to check the wine jars. "This is all the wine we have," she said. "This is terrible. The family will be embarrassed if we run out of wine. Ah, Jesus. I'll get him to help."

Mary told Jesus about the wine.

Jesus replied, *"Dear woman, why are you telling me this? It is not yet time for me to begin my work."* [11]

Mary looked at the servants and said, "Do whatever Jesus tells you to do."

The other two servants took a couple of steps backward. I looked at them, at Jesus, and at Mary, and I waited for orders.

Jesus said, *"Fill the water pots with water"* [12]

After many trips to the well, the water pots were full again. Each pot held about twenty or thirty gallons of water. Then Jesus commanded *"Now dip out some water and take it to the man in charge of the feast."* [13]

One servant said, "Not me; somebody else do it. I'm in trouble for getting the robes wet with soapy water. I'm not taking a dipper of water to the Master of Ceremonies."

"I'm not looking for more trouble. I'm in trouble for drinking some of the wine behind the myrtle bush," the other servant said. "The Master of Ceremonies can yell at someone else."

Suddenly, I was alone; the other servants had vanished. I scooped liquid out of the jar and filled a cup. "Excuse me, sir," I said to the Master of Ceremonies. "Please taste this wine before I serve it to the guests."

He took a sip and then another. Licking his lips, he motioned for the groom. "This is wonderful wine. It's not too sweet and not too dry. I've never tasted better wine. Why are you serving the best wine last?"

As I continued to serve the wine, I saw Susanna talking to Jesus. Curious me, I carried my tray of wine cups toward her. She glanced in my direction, saw the wine, shook her head, and motioned for me to go away. What a change. When I served Susanna previously, she never would have turned down a cup of wine.

The wedding feast lasted late into the night with music, poetry readings, dancing, feasting, and over one hundred gallons of fine wine. Changing water to wine was Jesus' first miracle, and I was part of it. Eloooree!

Throughout Jesus' ministry, Susanna and Joanna provided for Jesus and his disciples. Mary Magdalene and several other women also supported Jesus' ministry. Mary Magdalene had been very sick in body and in mind, and Jesus healed her. Several times I saw these women in the crowds surrounding Jesus.

Sea of Galilee

SAAs don't always get glamorous assignments. Spero and I were sitting at Meditation Point when we both felt a tingle and opened a hologram of fishermen and two boats full of fish. "I think we're going to clean fish," I said to Spero.

"Well, it won't be the first time," Spero answered.

"Elooooree!" we yelled and headed toward the Sea of Galilee.

As we landed, we took on the form of teenage boys and headed toward the water. People were running down the road. What were they running toward or from? Spero caught up with one of the men. "Where's everybody going?" he asked.

"We're going to hear the new teacher down by the lake," the man replied.

"He's not just a teacher; he's a miracle worker. My cousin's daughter was blind. He touched her eyes, and now she can see," another man said.

"He's better than John the Baptist," a boy said. "Come on, you don't want to miss him."

"What's his name?" I asked.

"Jesus," all three replied.

"Let's go listen to Jesus," I said to Spero.

"Our orders are to help fisherman, not listen to Jesus," Spero replied.

"They may be at the same cove," I said. "On to the lake."

"On to the lake," Spero sighed. "Remember we are here to help fishermen with two boats full of fish." We headed down the road and around a curve. There was a big crowd, and Jesus was standing at the water's edge. The crowd was so excited that they almost pushed Jesus into the lake.

"Look, fishermen," I said.

"Look, empty boats," Spero pointed out.

"Jesus is talking to one of the fishermen. Let's see what happens," I begged.

"Do you think fish are going to jump into their boats?" Spero said as he started down the road. "Come on, we have a job to do."

"I just want to listen to Jesus for a bit," I pleaded.

"Felix, you're going to get into trouble. Stay here. I'll go look for our fishermen. After I find them, I'll come get you. I'm not cleaning all those fish by myself."

Spero started down the road, and I sat down to listen to Jesus. I would need to work extra hard cleaning fish when Spero came back.

A large fisherman named Peter helped Jesus into his boat. The boat drifted away from shore, and Jesus began to teach. The four fishermen sat on rocks and held the ropes that kept the boat from drifting too far from shore.

After Jesus had dismissed the crowd, he said to Peter, *"Take the boat into the deep water. If all of you will put your nets into the water, you will catch some fish."* [14]

Peter and the others pulled the boat to shore. Peter pointed to the pile of wet, dirty nets. "Sir, we fished all night and caught nothing, absolutely nothing, not one fish, nada, but because you say to try, we will."

Peter and his brother, Andrew, were in one boat. The brothers James and John were in the other boat with their youngest brother, Jakob. They rowed the boats into deep water. As soon as Peter and Andrew let down their net, it jerked and started to break. "James! John! Jakob! Help!" Peter yelled. "We're going down!"

James, John, and Jakob strained at the oars until they reached Peter and Andrew. The five men pulled and pulled until they emptied the net into the boats. Both boats were so full of fish that they struggled to row to shore.

Peter looked at the fish and looked at Jesus. Peter covered his face with his hands and fell on his knees. "I'm sinful; go away," he said.

Jesus answered Peter, *"Don't be afraid. From now on your work will be to bring in people, not fish!"* [15]

Spero returned, "I didn't find our fishermen."

"I did. Look—fishermen and two boats loaded with fish," I said.

"Way to go, Felix," Spero said. "You were right to stop and listen to Jesus."

Jesus walked away, and the fishermen started to follow. They looked back at the fish and turned around. Spero yelled, "Go with Jesus! We will clean and salt your fish."

"Don't worry about anything—fish, boats, or nets. Just go with Jesus," I added.

Jesus turned and motioned for them to come. Peter, Andrew, James, and John nodded to us and hurried after Jesus. They walked around the curve and out of sight. Jakob stood on the beach and watched his brothers leave.

"Go with Jesus," Spero said. "We've got this."

"No, this is my father's business," Jakob said. "I must stay here. I can't believe James and John just left."

"Jakob, the best decision is to follow Jesus," I said. "Go with Jesus."

"No, there is too much work to do," Jakob answered as he pulled out his knife and started to clean fish. Spero and I joined him.

We sorted and cleaned fish—so many fish. After rubbing salt on them, we spread the nets on the beach to dry and mended holes. We pulled the boats on to the beach, washed them, and turned them over to dry.

This was a day of fun and pain. Jakob knew so many jokes that he had Spero and me laughing all day long. The pain came from the aching muscles, the salt-dried skin, and the nauseating smell of fish. We finally finished, and I fell to the sand and looked at the night sky. We lay on the beach all night, just enjoying God's creation. Spero and I don't see the sky from this side very often. It was glorious.

Several days later, we sold the fish and gave the money to Jakob for the families.

Over the hill, Eloooree! flip, flip, flip, and back to heaven.

Jesus chose twelve men to travel with him. These men were called disciples, and Peter, Andrew, James, and John were the first chosen. The disciples were an interesting group. At least four were fisherman, one was a rebel against Rome, and one worked as a tax collector for Rome. These men walked the land of Israel and sailed the Sea of Galilee with Jesus. They slept together, ate together, and learned together. They heard Jesus teach and saw his miracles. The disciples were privileged to be so close to him. No SAA could claim that privilege.

Jakob had a chance to be a disciple. He didn't make a bad decision, but he didn't make the best one. He did join his brothers from time to time and became a follower but not a disciple of Jesus.

Capernaum

I was returning from worship at the Crystal Sea when I felt a tingle and pulled up a hologram of crippled man lying on a mat. I recognized the city of Capernaum, a big city. How would I find this man in that city? I leaped into the cosmos and headed for Capernaum.

The city was crowded with people who had come to hear Jesus. I scanned the crowd, but I didn't see my crippled man. I looked down one side street, then another, then another one. Then I saw three men carrying a crippled man lying on a mat. They almost dropped him twice. "Can I help?" I yelled.

"Yes, please," the man carrying the front of the mat said. "We need to get our friend to Jesus."

I grabbed the left front corner of the mat. I thought, *This is going to be an easy assignment. Just carry the mat to Jesus, the man will be healed, and I can go back to heaven.*

We turned a corner and found the street clogged with people. Everyone wanted to see Jesus. We asked people to let us through, but no one heard us. Two of the friends tried to push their way through the crowd. People pushed back. We put the man down and stretched our hands and arms.

"Any ideas?" one friend asked.

"Let's go to the back of the house. Maybe we can get in there," the crippled man suggested.

We picked up the mat and edged and pushed our way to the back of the house. It was crowded back there, too. We laid the man down again and formed a wall around him so no one would step on him.

"Maybe we can wait until night," one friend suggested.

"We may have to, but it looks like rain," the leader said. "We're too close to give up. Think, men, think."

"Look, there are stairs on the back of the house. Do you think we could get on the roof?" I asked.

"Yes, but what good would that do? We'd still be outside and Jesus inside," one of the friends answered.

"We could make a hole in the roof and lower your friend down to Jesus," I suggested.

"Umm, that might work, but we need a rope."

"I'll get a rope. You get to the stairs," the leader said as he started down the street.

Soon, the leader returned with a rope and a chisel. Carrying the crippled man up the stairs was hard. To keep the mat level, those in the front had to hold the mat near their feet; those in the back had to hold the mat above their heads. We almost dropped the crippled man several times.

When we reached the roof, we started chipping away at it. Those listening to Jesus yelled at us to be quiet so they could hear him. We kept chipping away. CHIP, CHIP, CHIP.

The owner of the house yelled at us to stop or he would call the police. CHIP, CHIP, CHIP.

The people in the house yelled at us when chunks of the ceiling started falling on their heads. CHIP, CHIP, CHIP.

The people outside the house looked at us as if we were crazy. CHIP, CHIP, CHIP.

Finally, the hole was big enough. We tied ropes to the mat and lowered the crippled man into the house. A couple of the disciples guided the mat to the ground in front of Jesus.

Jesus looked at the man and said, *"Friend, your sins are forgiven."* [16]

The religious leaders coughed and squirmed, but they said nothing. Then I heard one teacher whisper, "How dare this man say such a thing? Only God can forgive sins."

Jesus looked at the religious leaders and said, *"Why do you have these questions in your minds? The Son of Man has power on earth to forgive sins. But how can I prove this to you? Maybe you are thinking it was easy for me to say, 'Your sins are forgiven.' There's no proof that it really happened. But what if I say to the man, 'Stand up and walk'? Then you will be able to see that I really have this power."* [17]

Jesus looked down at the crippled man and said, *"I tell you, stand up! Take your mat and go home!"* [18]

The man moved his legs, rolled over, and rose to his hands and knees. A disciple helped the man stand. He took one step, then two. He smiled, looked up at his friends, and said, "Thank you." He bowed to Jesus and whispered, "Praise God! Thank you."

He rolled up his mat and walked out of the house. The crowd parted for him as if he were a king, but he was a walking miracle. Most of the people left praising God, but the religious leaders murmured against Jesus.

I spent the next three days repairing the roof with the three friends. SAAs always leave things as good as or better than we found them. The homeowner, who at first was mad at us for making a hole in his roof, was delighted with his new one.

As I left town, I heard the laughter of a party. I peeked in and saw the formerly crippled man showing his friends how he could dance. With a smile, Eloooree! and a triple somersault, I returned to heaven.

Galilee

I felt as if I were playing "Where is my person?" today. A woman who had been sick for twelve years needed help to reach Jesus. And I was her help.

I landed near the Sea of Galilee where a large crowd surrounded Jesus. How was I going to find my woman? I knew she was sick, so I'd look for a sick woman. I started working my way through the crowd. I looked at every woman. None of them appeared to be sick.

My "sick woman" plan wasn't working. What had she looked like in the hologram? She had on a brown robe. Most of the women wore brown robes.

Her hair was covered by a scarf. Every woman's hair was covered by a scarf—brown or gray. My woman wore a black scarf. Now I was on the hunt for a black scarf. I pushed back into the crowd. Who was wearing a black scarf?

Suddenly, the crowd parted for a man running up the road. I knew him. He was Jairus, a leader of the nearby synagogue. Six years before, he and I put out a fire in a barley field.

I met Jairus on this very road. I was beating out a barley fire with my robe when he came running up. "I thought I smelled burning barley!" he shouted. "I'll attack the fire from the other side."

Jairus yanked off his robe and started beating the fire from the other direction. Up, down, up, down, we went over and over again. Finally, the fire was out. We both fell to the ground exhausted. I was rubbing my aching arms, and he was stretching his sore fingers.

"I'm Felix," I said. "Thanks for the help."

"I'm Jairus. I'm glad we put the fire out. The man who owns this field is poor and needs a good harvest," he replied.

As we stood up, Jairus sniffed the air. He looked at his robe, burned and covered in soot. "My wife

is going to be upset. She just finished making
this robe for me. She wanted me to wait until the
Sabbath to wear it, but I had to wear it today."

"Here, take her some flowers," I said as I picked
some beautiful wildflowers.

"It's worth a try," Jairus chuckled. "Even if my wife
doesn't like them, my six-year-old daughter will.
She loves flowers. If you are still in town, come to
the synagogue on the Sabbath."

"I'm just passing through. I'll be far away by that
time," I said. "Shalom."

I wondered what Jairus wanted with Jesus today.

When Jairus reached Jesus, he fell to his knees and
said, "Sir, my only daughter is dying. Please come
and heal her."

Oh, the little girl who loves flowers is sick, I thought.

Jesus motioned for Jairus to lead the way. As they
were walking away, I realized I was enjoying
wonderful memories when I should have been
looking for the woman in the black scarf. Now
everyone was moving and following Jesus. Where
was my woman in the black scarf?

I looked in front of me, behind me, to the right, and
to the left. Where was my woman? Then I spotted a

bit of black bobbing on the other side of the crowd. I needed to get over there. "Excuse me ... pardon me ... please let me through," I said over and over.

I finally reached the other side and heard a woman muttering to herself, "If I can just touch his clothes, that will be enough to heal me."

I had found my woman, but Jesus was moving farther and farther away from her. She was too sick to push through the crowd. I stepped in front of her. I felt her weak fists pounding on my back. "Move! I need to get to Jesus," she said.

"Stay close to me; I'll get you to Jesus," I said. She grabbed the back of my robe, and we slowly made our way through the crowd. When we were close to Jesus, I stepped back so she could reach him. She touched the hem of his robe.

A smile spread across her face as she stood up. "I'm healed; I know I'm healed," she whispered.

At that moment, Jesus turned around and looked at the crowd. He asked, *"Who touched me?"* [19]

Peter said, "Master, in this big crowd, anyone could have bumped against you."

Jesus replied, *"Someone touched me. I felt power go out from me."* [20]

I nudged the woman forward. Trembling, she whispered, "Please, be merciful." Falling at Jesus' feet, she told in a frightened voice how she had touched his robe and had been healed.

Jesus helped her up and said, *"My daughter, you are made well because you believed. Go in peace."* [21]

A man walked up to Jairus and said, "I'm sorry, sir. Your daughter has died. There is no need to bother the teacher."

Jairus' eyes filled with tears as he looked at Jesus. Jesus said, *"Don't be afraid! Just believe and your daughter will be well."* [22]

My mission was finished, so I left the crowd. Eloooree! flip, flip, flip, and back to heaven.

I watched to see what would happen to Jairus' daughter, the girl who loved flowers.

Jairus led Jesus to his house. As they approached, Jairus gasped when he heard the sounds of wailing and mourning. Jesus stepped forward and said, *"Don't cry. She is not dead. She is only sleeping."* [23]

The wailing turned to laughter and the mourning to scorn. Jairus hugged his wife and introduced her to Jesus. They led Jesus to their daughter's room. Jesus took the girl's hand and said, *"Little girl, stand up!"* [24]

The girl blinked her eyes a couple of times, smiled at her father, and sat on the edge of the bed. Without any help, she stood up and started walking—no, skipping—around the room. Jairus wiped tears from his eyes, and his wife hugged him and their daughter. Jesus watched the celebration and then reminded the parents that their daughter needed food after being so sick.

I was rejoicing in the healing of Jairus' daughter when the commander approached. "Felix, you're back to your old habits. You're watching Earth instead of writing your reports."

"Sir, I was going to write my report as soon as I saw what happened with the little girl," I said.

"The girl wasn't your mission; Jairus wasn't your mission. The sick woman was your mission," the commander replied. "Write your report now, and when you're finished..."

"I know, I know, proofreading and fact checking," I grumbled."

"No, Felix, review recent records for people we can encourage to listen to Jesus, but maybe I should reconsider and give you the other assignment," the commander said.

"Please, sir, let me review records. I'll start my report right now," I said as I clapped my hands to bring up the database. When I finished the review, my list included Joab (he was grown up now), Susanna, Joanna, Jakob, and many others, including Barabbas. His record wasn't encouraging, but I still hoped he would change. Listening to Jesus would make the difference.

Hillside in Galilee

SAAs frequently appear as traveling merchants.
Today, I went to Galilee as a seller of fish. I sold
fresh fish and would grill some for passing travelers.
The day started early, and I quickly sold my fish.
By midmorning, I had only five left. A mother and
her son bought three of them. I offered her the last
two. The mother refused and said to give them to
someone in need.

Her son pointed to a very tall man running down
the road. "Here comes Uncle Aram!" he shouted.

When Uncle Aram reached us, he exclaimed, "If
Amos wants to hear Jesus, we must go now! Jesus is

in that boat close to the coast. We must go now or lose sight the boat."

"I must fix something for you to eat," the boy's mother replied.

"No time. We must go," Uncle Aram argued.

"Grill those two fish," the mother said to me. Looking at Uncle Aram, she said, "Stay here. I'll go get five barley loaves I made yesterday. I'll be back before the fish are grilled, and you can be on your way."

The mother hurried down the road while Uncle Aram helped me grill the fish. She returned with the barley loaves just as I finished grilling. She threw the fish into a scarf holding the loaves and gave the bundle to Amos. The boy and Uncle Aram hurried down the road toward the coast.

I gave my stall to another fish seller; he needed a new stall. My adventure over, I walked over a hill to return to heaven. I felt a tingle and opened a hologram of the boy giving Jesus his bundle. I had a new mission. I dashed to the coast road and hurried after Uncle Aram and Amos.

Jesus' boat pulled into a cove and he climbed out. After walking up a hill, Jesus sat down and motioned for the crowd to sit. Thousands of people sat down to listen to him. How was I going to find my young boy in this crowd?

I sniffed but smelled sheep instead of fish. I spotted Philos sitting next to a shepherd holding his crook. The odor of sheep clung to the shepherd, so not many people sat near Philos. He winked at me.

I heard a boy's voice and turned to see if it was Amos. I saw Spero helping a family with several small children. Spero was too busy watching the children to notice me. Yael was here, but no Susanna. I also spotted Jakob, but where was Amos?

I saw a very tall man in the crowd. I had found Uncle Aram and Amos. I sat down next to the boy and said, "Hello, do you remember me from the fish market?" Amos nodded his head yes and pointed toward Jesus.

Jesus was speaking about God's love. I was listening to Jesus when I heard a voice behind me shout, "Look at this crowd! Who could love this ragtag bunch of losers?"

I looked behind me, and there sat Slimatus, one of Satan's demons. He didn't look like a demon; he was dressed as a farmer. I scanned the crowd and identified several more demons. They were coughing, talking, scratching—anything to keep people from hearing Jesus. Slimatus knew I was an SAA and stuck his fists up to fight. I felt my fists tighten. I took a deep breath and relaxed my fists. I could defeat him in any fight, but that's not how SAAs settle problems. I turned my attention to Jesus.

Jesus spoke about loving one another and helping each other. Slimatus yelled, "Why would anyone help these people? They're sitting here doing nothing when they should be at work. What lazy bums!"

Several in the group shouted, "Be quiet! We want to hear Jesus."

"Fools!" Slimatus replied.

Jesus motioned for his disciples to come to him. He told them something. The disciples pointed at the crowd and shook their heads. Jesus said something, and the disciples walked into the crowd. Andrew walked toward us.

I looked at Amos and asked, "Do you have the lunch your mother prepared?"

"Here in this scarf," he said as he patted the bundle in his lap.

"Could you share some of your food with me?" I said. "I didn't bring anything to eat."

"No, there's only enough for Uncle Aram and me," he replied.

"That's right, son. You'll go hungry if you share," Slimatus growled. I turned around, and he gave me a nasty smile. I couldn't let Slimatus upset me.

Andrew asked if we had any food. I whispered to Amos, "Tell Andrew about your bread and fish."

"No, there's not enough to share," Amos said.

"That's right. Keep your mouth shut; Jesus would love to take that food from you," Slimatus whispered.

Andrew went through the crowd, but no one gave him any food.

"Give the food to Andrew. He's probably hungry," I encouraged Amos.

"Andrew should have brought his own food," Amos replied, wrapping his arms around the bread and fish.

"Right again, son," Slimatus said. "You shouldn't go hungry because he didn't think ahead."

"Jesus won't let you go hungry. Ask Andrew if he is going to give the food to Jesus," I suggested.

"Okay, I'll talk to Andrew, but he should have brought his own food," Amos answered.

"Don't do it, son. You'll be sorry," Slimatus said.

I motioned for Andrew to come over and introduced Amos.

"Jesus wants to feed this crowd," Andrew told us.

"I only have two fish and five loaves," Amos said.

"Let's take them to Jesus and see what he does," Andrew said.

"Don't do it! You're going to be hungry!" Slimatus yelled.

Jesus spoke to Amos, and the boy gave Jesus the food.

I turned around to give Slimatus a big smile, but he had left.

After Jesus gave thanks for the food, the disciples gave bread and fish to over five thousand people. Amos told anyone who would listen about meeting Jesus. He talked so much that he forgot about being hungry, but he and everyone else had enough to eat.

My job was finished. I left the crowd before the bread and fish were distributed and returned to heaven with a big Eloooree!

Fifty years later: Today I served at a big family party. A man was celebrating his sixtieth birthday. He sat under his grape arbor and told his many grandchildren about the day Jesus used his two fish and five loaves to fed 5,000 people. This man was Amos all grown up. I whispered Eloooree!

Northern Israel

*P*hilos and I were heading to Meditation Point when we spotted a dazzling light coming from planet Earth. I had never seen a light like this on any of the planets. It was brighter than the birth of a star. It was more beautiful than a sunrise. It was more brilliant than a flash of lightning. It was the glory of heaven. The light was coming from a mountain.

"I remember this light," Philos said. "Do you?"

"Of course—it's the light of God's Spirit. We saw it cover Mary and Anne in Nazareth."

"And on Mount Sinai."

"And at the dedication of the temple in Jerusalem."

"Eloooree! Eloooree!" we yelled as we flipped and spun around. Other angels came rushing to see why we were so excited.

Jesus was on the mountain with Peter, James, and John. Suddenly, Moses and Elijah were talking with Jesus. Heaven and Earth were meeting on this mountain. The glory of heaven surrounded Jesus, Moses, and Elijah.

We shouted, "Eloooree! Eloooree!"

Peter looked from Jesus to Moses to Elijah and back at Jesus. He shook his head and turned to Jesus. "I can't believe what I'm seeing," Peter said. "It's incredible, amazing, and beyond belief. Let's build three shelters: one for you, one for Moses, and one for Elijah."

John tugged at Peter's sleeve. Peter looked down and saw John pointing at the ground. James and John were kneeling. Peter dropped to his knees. James and John were right—surrounded by the glory of heaven, kneeling was the only thing to do. The angels knelt.

A cloud descended over the mountain. God's voice came from the cloud saying, *This is my Son, the one I love. I am very pleased with him. Obey him!"* [25]

The disciples bowed their heads to the ground in worship and fear. Angels bowed their heads in adoration.

The cloud lifted. Moses and Elijah returned to heaven. Jesus touched Peter, James, and John and said, *"Stand up. Don't be afraid."* [26]

Jesus led them down the mountain. What a glimpse of glory. Eloooree!

Angels watched as Moses and Elijah returned to heaven. We wondered if they would bring a message from Jesus. They said nothing, but they headed to the Crystal Sea to worship. Singing praises, the angels followed them.

Jerusalem

I was in the market in Jerusalem buying clay to fix a widow's roof. I heard Jesus' voice, and my curiosity got the best of me—I had to go listen to him. He was about to tell a story; I'd never been in the crowd when Jesus told one. I hoped I wouldn't get into trouble for stopping.

A lawyer asked Jesus, "If I'm to love my neighbor as myself, who is my neighbor?"

Jesus answered this question with the story of the Good Samaritan.

A Samaritan was someone who lived in an area between Jerusalem and Nazareth. At one time, only Jews lived in this area, but now lots of people lived there. Samaritans and Jews disliked each other and avoided meeting. Most Jews could not imagine a good Samaritan.

Jesus said, *"A man was going down the road from Jerusalem to Jericho. Some robbers surrounded him, tore off his clothes, and beat him. Then they left him lying there on the ground almost dead."* [27]

A Jewish priest came by but moved to the other side of the road when he saw the injured man. He did not want to get involved. Then a Levite (or temple assistant) came down the road. He was late, so he rushed past the injured man. He didn't have time to help.

A Samaritan saw the injured man and knelt down beside him. The Samaritan wiped the injured man's wounds with healing oil and wrapped them with bandages. Then he lifted the injured man onto his donkey. They moved slowly until they reached an inn. The Samaritan took care of the injured man until the next morning.

The Samaritan gave money to the innkeeper to take care of the injured man. "Take good care of this man. If you spend more than what I gave you, I will repay you," the Samaritan said to the innkeeper.

Jesus asked the lawyer, *"Which one of these three men do you think was really a neighbor to the man who was hurt by the robbers?"* [28]

The lawyer looked at his friends, coughed, and tugged at the fringe on his prayer shawl. Looking at his feet, he whispered, "The one who helped him."

He didn't like that the Samaritan was the hero of the story. Most Jews didn't think Samaritans could be heroes. Jesus taught that God cares for everyone, and so should we. Most Jewish leaders didn't think God should care for Gentiles (non-Jews) like Samaritans.

I hurried to the widow's house to fix her roof, but I thought about the story. SAAs are sent to help everyone, because God loves everyone.

When I arrived back in heaven, Lt. Parebo and I walked to the Crystal Sea to worship together. "Did you enjoy Jesus' story?" he asked.

"You saw me listening? I'm sorry; he tells such good stories, and I did finish my mission," I replied.

"Don't be concerned, Felix. You'll never get in trouble for listening to Jesus," Lt. Parebo answered.

"Eloooree," I whispered.

Bethany

I get to be a girl today and encourage a woman to listen to Jesus, my favorite thing to do.

I landed in Bethany, a town near Jerusalem. How would I find this special woman? In the hologram, she was wearing a tan robe with a brown belt and was standing in a kitchen. Everyone here was wearing a tan robe with a brown belt. As I wandered down the street looking at the people, a woman asked, "Do you want to work today? I need someone to help me in the kitchen."

"Yes, ma'am. I'm a good cook," I answered. I found my woman, or she found me.

"My sister and I will do all the cooking, but I need someone to carry produce from the market and keep the cook fires going. You will need to turn the spit to roast the goat. Are you interested?"

"Yes, ma'am."

Martha, her sister Mary, and their brother Lazarus were friends of Jesus. They had invited family and friends to hear Jesus teach and stay for dinner afterward. Martha was planning a very fancy dinner: roast goat with mint sauce, pumpkin stew, bread, fresh fruit, dried figs, and raisins.

She selected pumpkins for the stew. It took me several trips to lug the pumpkins to the house. Many of the herbs she needed grew in the backyard, but not mint. She needed to go to a local meadow to pick mint for her special sauce.

Everyone would eat on the roof where there was a cool breeze. I swept the roof, helped carry tables and benches to the roof, and erected a canopy over the tables. I cleaned the dishes and cups and started a fire to roast the goat.

While Martha was getting the meat from the market, Mary said she wanted to listen to Jesus. She went into the house and sat next to Lazarus at Jesus' feet. Martha saw Mary listening to Jesus and shook her head. "She'll listen for a bit, and then she'll help me. She knows this is an important dinner."

"Wouldn't you like to listen to Jesus?" I asked. "I can turn the spit to cook the goat and stir the stew. You could buy bread in the market. Goat, pumpkin stew, and bread would be a wonderful meal."

"No, that would never do. Jesus is a special guest, and I want the meal to be perfect. I'll start the bread now, and then I'll get flowers and fruit from the market to decorate the tables. When I return, I'll make my special mint sauce for the goat."

When Martha returned from the market, I said, "Ma'am, you go listen to Jesus; I'll finish the bread. The stew is finished and the goat is almost ready. I can do what needs to be done."

"I'm going to decorate the tables, and you ask Mary to go pick mint so I can make the special sauce. Normally she isn't lazy, but today she just sits around and lets me do all the work."

"Do you want me to pick the mint?" I asked.

"No, Mary knows the mint I like."

I didn't bother Mary; she was doing what God wanted her to do. I kept turning the spit, stirring the stew, and watching the bread. Taking dried figs and raisin cakes out of a jar, Martha asked, "Has Mary gone to get the mint?"

"No, ma'am," I said. "Do you want me to go?"

"No, Mary should be helping. I'm going to talk to Jesus about this."

"Please don't," I said too late.

Martha had gone into the house and I heard her saying, "Lord, don't you care that my sister has left me to do the work? Tell her to help me!"

Jesus looked up and said, *"Martha, Martha, you are getting worried and upset about too many things. Only one thing is important. Mary has made the right choice, and it will never be taken away from her."* [29]

Martha stumbled back to the kitchen and plopped down on a bench. "I just wanted to make everything perfect for Jesus." She covered her face with her hands.

I filled a cup with water and gave it to her. Kneeling beside her, I said, "Ma'am, your presence makes the meal perfect, not roast goat or pumpkin stew—not even your special mint sauce."

"I feel like such a fool. How can I ever face Jesus again?"

"Oh, ma'am, all he wants is for you to listen to him. Rinse your face. Go to him."

Martha splashed water on her face and dried it on a towel. I straightened her veil and pushed a few stray hairs behind her ears. She eased into the house. Mary and Lazarus squeezed over so she could sit between them. Mary gave her a hug and Jesus patted her shoulder.

When Mary gave me the sign, I took the platters of goat meat, bowls of pumpkin stew, and baskets of bread to the tables on the roof, but no special mint sauce. Jesus thanked God for the food. What a party. Martha couldn't have asked for more— wonderful food and better conversation.

Jesus laughed and talked to his friends and even to the serving girl. Jesus knew who I was, but when the Lord of the Universe smiled at me, it was amazing. I almost let my angel identity slip out, but I kept my cool, bowed my head, smiled, and quietly hummed.

After the meal, Jesus went off to pray, Martha napped, and Mary helped me clean the kitchen. Lazarus paid me for my work. Usually, I don't take money, but this time I did. As I walked out of Bethany, I handed several beggars the coins.

Around the next corner, I yelled Eloooree! leaped into the cosmos, and headed for Meditation Point.

The commander met me when I arrived. "Good job, Felix. I was concerned when Jesus smiled at you, but you stayed calm. Making progress," he said.

"Thank you, sir," I replied. "I enjoyed being so close to him."

The Road to Bethel

Today I had another chance to hear Jesus teach by telling a story. I was accompanying a young man from Jerusalem to Bethel when I heard Jesus' voice.

"Let's go hear the teacher," I suggested.

"No, I want to go home," the young man replied. "I've been listening to teachers in Jerusalem. I've had enough. Always do this; don't ever do that. Never have any fun."

"This teacher is different. Everybody is talking about him."

"Who is he?"

"Jesus, the teacher, the miracle worker, the Savior. Let's listen to him until the sun drops below that tree. If you don't want to listen anymore, we'll leave."

"Promise we'll leave?"

"Yes, come on."

We walked to the bottom of a hill where Jesus was seated. A large crowd surrounded him. Some in the crowd were Jewish teachers who complained that Jesus should not spend time with liars, thieves, and other sinners. Jesus replied by telling the story of the Lost Son (or Prodigal Son).

Jesus said, *"There was a man who had two sons. The younger son said to his father, 'Give me now the part of your property that I am supposed to receive someday.' So, the father divided his wealth between his two sons."* [30]

By asking for part of the family fortune, the younger son was saying to his father, "I wish you were dead," but the father gave the younger son the money he wanted.

The younger son took his money and traveled to another country. He spent his money on friends, fun, and foolishness. After his money was gone, he no longer had any friends or fun, and he felt like a fool. Soon, he was hungry and broke. He found a job, but it wasn't a good one. He had to feed pigs. One day as he fed the pigs, he looked at their garbage and thought, "I'm hungry enough to eat this garbage. If I were a servant at my father's house, I would have plenty to eat. I know what I did was wrong, but I want to go home. I can't be my father's son anymore, but maybe he'll hire me as a servant." That day, he headed home.

The sun dropped below the top of the tree. "Do you want to stay or go?" I asked the young man.

"Shh, Jesus is speaking, I wonder what the father will do," he said. We settled down to hear the rest of the story.

The father saw his son staggering down the road in the distance. Running to his son, the father hugged and kissed him. The son said, "Father, I have sinned against God and hurt you. I am not worthy to be called your son."

The father hugged him harder and called to the servants, "Bring the best robe and put it on him. Put a ring on his finger and sandals on his feet. Tonight, we will celebrate. My son was dead, but now he lives. He was lost, but now he is found."

"Wow, the father took the son back. I don't know if my father would take me back if I'd behaved badly," the young man said to me.

"Many earthly fathers wouldn't take their sons back, but your heavenly father will if you admit that you have done wrong," I replied.

I was amazed when I heard the teachers talking. They didn't like the idea that God would forgive sinners. Why was it so hard for them to understand that God loves them?

Soon we were in Bethel. The young man was welcomed by his father, mother, brothers, and sisters. They even included me in a "welcome home" celebration. I hoped my young man knew that God loved him even more than his earthly father did.

After the celebration, I left town and leapt into the cosmos. I went to the Crystal Sea. There I joined the other angels in praising God for his love.

Bethany

W hat a surprise! SAAs don't usually get to help the same people again, but I was sent back to Martha's house. This time, I was a young man looking for work in Bethany. Lazarus hired me to help around the house. I cut wood, fetched water from the well in town, and carried produce from the market. Lazarus and his sisters treated me well. I had plenty to eat, I slept inside, and they gave me clothes. Lazarus wanted me to help him, so he taught me to do math.

One day, Martha yelled, "Mary, come quick, and bring Felix with you!"

We ran into the house. Lazarus was lying on the floor. He was hot and unconscious. I laid him on his bed. Mary brewed some herbal tea, but it didn't help. Lazarus got sicker. Martha rubbed some healing oils on him, but it didn't help. Lazarus got even sicker. I washed him with a cool cloth, but it didn't help. Lazarus got sicker still.

After several days, Martha said, "Felix, go find Jesus. Tell him Lazarus is sick. Hurry!"

I found Jesus and told him about Lazarus. I expected Jesus to return to Bethany with me, but he sent me back alone.

Mary and Martha started to cry when I arrived without Jesus. They knew he loved Lazarus and could heal him. We made more tea, rubbed on more oil, and bathed Lazarus in cool water, but nothing helped. Two days later, he died. The sisters buried Lazarus in a tomb in a cave. Several men pushed a large rock over the cave's entrance.

So much sadness filled the house. People came from as far away as Jerusalem to comfort Martha and Mary. The sisters didn't notice the people. They sat in a dark corner and prayed. I made their favorite foods, but they wouldn't eat. I didn't know how to help them. Then a visitor brought news that Jesus was coming. Martha ran out the door and down the road. Mary told me to follow her.

Martha found Jesus and said, "Lord, if only you had come, my brother would still be alive. Ask God, and Lazarus will live even now."

Jesus said to her, *"I am the resurrection. I am life. Everyone who believes in me will have life, even if they die. And everyone who lives and believes in me will never really die. Martha, do you believe this?"* [31]

Martha answered, "Yes, Lord, you are the Savior." Then she got Mary, and they walked with Jesus to the tomb of Lazarus.

When they arrived at the tomb, Jesus stood there as tears ran down his cheeks. Then he said, *"Move the stone away."* [32]

Martha, always practical, stepped in front of the stone and said, "Lord, my brother has been dead four days; the smell will be bad."

Jesus eased Martha away from the stone and motioned for the stone to be moved. I helped the men roll the stone away from the tomb. Jesus looked to heaven and shouted, *"Lazarus, come out!"* [33]

Everyone looked at the tomb. We heard groaning and shuffling. Then a figure appeared at the entrance to the cave. Mary and Martha gasped and stepped back. Lazarus, wrapped in a sheet, came stumbling out of the cave.

Jesus said to the people, *"Take off the cloth and let him go."* [34]

Everyone in Bethany crowded into the house to see Lazarus. Friends rejoiced with Martha and Mary. Martha worried about how to feed so many people. Jesus smiled at Martha, and she nodded. She put out bread, fruit, and cheese. She thanked Jesus, talked to her guests, and kept Lazarus close to her. What a wonderful celebration we had!

Many people hurried off to spread the good news. However, a few people hurried off to tell the high priest what had happened. They felt that Jesus was dangerous. I returned to heaven to praise God.

Jericho

A s I left the Crystal Sea, Lt. Parebo appeared beside me. "Hello, Felix. I have finished reviewing your latest entries. They were entered quickly and completely," he said.

"Thank you, sir. I'm learning it is best not to let reports pile up."

"Your next mission is a two-for-one. You will help two men see Jesus. One is a beggar, and the other is wealthy."

"Sounds interesting, sir. When do I leave?"

"Now, or you'll miss your first opportunity. By the way, you'll be a tax collector in training working with Zacchaeus," Lt. Parebo explained.

"Away I go, sir!" I yelled as I dove into the cosmos.

I landed near Jericho and saw a blind beggar sitting beside the road. Jesus, surrounded by a large crowd, came walking over the hill. The blind beggar shouted, "What is happening? Why all the noise?"

"Jesus of Nazareth is coming!" the people yelled.

The blind man leaped up and yelled, "Jesus, help me! Jesus, help me!"

People shouted, "Shh, don't bother the teacher!"

Here was a man who needed to see Jesus. He believed that Jesus could help him. I pushed my way toward him. He wasn't hard to find because he yelled louder and louder, "Jesus, help me! Jesus, help me!"

When I reached his side, I heard Jesus say, *"Bring that man to me!"* [35]

I asked the man his name. "Bartimaeus," he replied.

"Bartimaeus, hold on to my arm and let me guide you to Jesus," I replied. He gripped my arm, and we pushed our way through the crowd to Jesus.

Jesus asked, *"What do you want me to do for you?"* [36]

As he squeezed my arm harder, Bartimaeus said, "I want to see."

Jesus said, *"You can see now. You are healed because you believed."* [37]

Bartimaeus immediately saw Jesus; he saw the crowd, the trees, the road, the sun. He let go of my arm and raised his hands in the air as he shouted, "Hallelujah! Praise God!" He skipped along behind Jesus as the crowd continued toward Jericho.

I had accomplished half of my mission. Now to find Zacchaeus. He was a tax collector for the Romans in Jericho. A tax collector had to send a certain amount of money to Rome, but he could collect extra money for his own use. Most tax collectors were greedy and robbed people. They were rich, but hated.

I needed to hurry. I was going to be late for my first and probably only day as a tax collector in training. I ran down the main street in Jericho and through a large park. This was a rich neighborhood—big houses surrounded by high walls and streets lined with sycamore trees. I knocked on a door in one of the walls; a servant opened the door. He motioned that I should sit down, and then he disappeared.

Soon the tax collector's secretary motioned for me to follow him. Next to a large fountain sat Zacchaeus. He was short, but the fountain made him look even shorter. He wore a yellow robe of fine linen and a dark blue tunic with a red sash wrapped around his plump waist. His leather sandals were dyed a bright blue. On his hands were several rings, including his ring of office. This was a wealthy man.

He finished a peach he was eating and took a long hard look at me. "You're late."

"Sorry, sir. I was delayed coming into town," I said.

"Can you read and write and handle sums?" he growled at me.

"Yes, sir, of course I can." I replied.

"No 'of course' about it. The last assistant could barely write his name. He was a complete fool. I don't want another fool!" he yelled. "What's all that noise I hear? Are there games in town today? No one ever tells me anything."

"I don't believe that there are any games today; I think the people are going to hear a teacher," I replied. "The teacher is quite famous. He is Jesus of Nazareth. Have you heard of him?"

"I think so. Another tax collector, Matthew, joined his followers. Matthew will get tired of that life soon enough. Good food and wine, fine clothes and jewels, a soft bed, and bags of money—that's what a man wants," Zacchaeus said.

"It may be what a man wants, but not always what he needs," I replied.

"You sound like a foolish priest," Zacchaeus said as he shook his head.

I smiled.

"Normally, I don't worry much about religious things. Oh, the priests are always happy to see me. I give them money, and I get a seat up front so I can see," he mused as he walked around the fountain. "I would like to see this Jesus. Matthew found him interesting, so I might also find him interesting. It would be something different to do today."

He stared at me and said, "Your first job as my assistant is to buy me a seat right up front so I can see Jesus better than anyone else. You'd better hurry; I want a good seat."

"Jesus teaches on a hillside. The people sit on the ground and listen to him. They don't sell tickets to see him, and there aren't any reserved seats. He

FELIX & THE MESSIAH

wants everyone to be able to hear him. I'll think of a plan so you can see him," I replied.

"Whatever your plan is, remember this: I do not want to sit with the people. Now go figure something out. The crowd is getting louder; Jesus must be coming into Jericho."

I was beginning to understand my mission. I walked to the park and looked at the trees. I had an idea. Now to convince Zacchaeus.

"Jericho is filled with trees. If you sit in one of the trees, you would see everything, but the people wouldn't see you," I explained to Zacchaeus.

"Fool! Are you suggesting that I climb a tree? I am a dignified man wearing expensive clothes. I want neither my dignity nor my clothes ruined. Another fool; they've sent me another fool!"

"I'll give you my cotton robe to protect your clothes. If we go now, no one will see you climb the tree. I'll help you get up into the tree, and I'll keep people away. No one will know you're there. I don't know another way for you to see Jesus and not mix with the people."

"You'll help me and keep it a secret?" he asked. "I am curious about Jesus."

"Yes, I'll do my best to keep people from knowing you are in the tree. Let's get you in it before Jesus and the people come."

Zacchaeus and I hurried to the park. I gave Zacchaeus my cotton robe and held the ladder while he climbed the tree. As I was hiding the ladder, several boys rounded the corner yelling, "Jesus is coming! Jesus is coming!"

I stepped in front of the tree to keep people from getting close. Then I saw Jesus walking toward me. He stopped and looked up into the tree. He said, *"Zacchaeus, hurry! Come down! I must stay at your house today."* [38]

Zacchaeus started climbing down before I could grab the ladder to help him.

I followed and listened to the people grumble about Jesus being with a tax collector. I heard such phrases as "Doesn't Jesus know who Zacchaeus is?" "Why would Jesus waste time with a man like Zacchaeus?" "If Jesus will visit with a man like Zacchaeus, I don't want to know Jesus." I shook my head; they still didn't understand. My mission was finished, so with a triple somersault and a yell of Eloooree! I returned to heaven.

I had to know what happened to Zacchaeus. He was so happy to be with Jesus. I decided to watch for just a bit. A "bit" turned into all day because Zacchaeus threw a banquet for Jesus. He invited his friends: tax collectors and shady businessmen. After dinner, Zacchaeus told Jesus, "I have money and jewels, but I'm not happy. I'm going to help the poor of Jericho by giving them half of my things."

Everyone gasped, because Zacchaeus had lots of things.

"That's not all," Zacchaeus continued. "I have cheated people, and I will give them four times what I stole."

Everyone was shocked. This was not the Zacchaeus they knew. He had changed. Some even called Zacchaeus a fool.

Jesus replied, *"Today is the day for this family to be saved from sin. Yes, even this tax collector is one of God's chosen people. The Son of Man came to find lost people and save them."* [39]

I smiled as I started to update the records for Bartimaeus and Zacchaeus. Both men met Jesus and were changed.

Jerusalem

Passover was coming. Crowds surged into Jerusalem. Another busy Passover season—could anything be better? I was helping a family with seven young children set up their camp near the Mount of Olives. I heard shouting in the distance. It got louder and louder. People were singing praises. I drove the last tent stake into the ground and shouted, "Happy Passover!" I ran to the road going from Bethany to Jerusalem.

Jesus was coming to Jerusalem, riding on the back of a donkey. The crowd exploded into joy as he came closer. Some threw their coats on the ground, and others waved palm branches in the air.

Everyone shouted, "Praise him! Hallelujah! Here comes the King of Israel!"

SAA orders were not to worship Jesus while he was on Earth. Today, our orders changed; we could join the crowds praising Jesus. I ran to the road and shouted as loud as I could, "Hallelujah to the Lord Most High! Praise his glorious name!" As Jesus rode past me, I dropped to my knees and bowed my head. I jumped, leaped, and twirled. I tripped and fell flat on my back. The breath was knocked out of me, and I lay on the ground with my eyes closed. People rushed to help me. When I opened my eyes, they stepped back.

"Look at his eyes."

"Yellow stars."

"He's a demon!"

"Grab him."

"Stone him! Stone him!" people yelled as they picked up rocks.

"No, I'm not a demon!" I screamed as I tried to stand up.

"We'll take care of him," a temple guard said as he approached.

"We know what to do with his type," said his partner. They pulled me up and dragged me off the road and down a path.

Oh, this is bad, I thought. *What am I going to do now?*

When we reached a grove of trees, I looked at the temple guards. They were the commander and Lt. Parebo. *I might be better off with the temple guards,* I thought.

"Go! Go now, Felix!" the commander ordered. "I'll talk to you when I get back to heaven. Go!"

"I'm sor..." I started to say.

"Go, Felix. Go!"

I did a triple flip and leapt into the cosmos. When I landed in heaven, I raced to the Reflection Grotto. How had this happened? I'd been doing so well.

I heard angels praising God as they came back from Earth. I eased out to see what was happening on Earth. Sheep were braying, bird's wings were flapping, and money was scattering on the ground. An angel yelled, " Jesus is chasing the merchants out of the temple!"

I looked at the temple. Tables were turned over. Animals had broken out of their pens. Birds were flying everywhere. The merchants were grumbling to the priests.

"We should arrest Jesus," one merchant said.

"Not now. The people like him. His arrest might start a riot," a priest answered.

"We must do something. Look at the mess in the temple. Where is the chief priest?"

"I'm here. Calm down," he said. "Give me some time. Jesus will not be a problem much longer. I have a plan. The temple guard will take care of Jesus."

At the mention of the temple guard, I remembered the commander and Lt. Parebo. The commander was walking toward me. I stood up, straightened my shoulders, and waited for what was to come.

"Felix, I thought we had solved your problem. I must discuss what happened today with the Angelic Council. No more Earth missions for you," the commander said.

"I'm so sorry. I was so excited to be worshipping Jesus," I said. "Please let me do Earth missions again."

"We'll see what the Angelic Council says. I need you. I hear that this is going to be a very special

Passover. Work with Lt. Parebo until the council gives a ruling," the commander replied and walked away.

While I waited, I watched Jerusalem, usually by myself. Spero and Philos sat with me when they didn't have missions.

Satan and his demons were active in Jerusalem. Satan appeared to be a wealthy merchant, and the demons had many disguises. They spoke to citizens, pilgrims, priests, and even the leaders at the temple. Their message was that Jesus must die.

When Jesus went to pray, the disciples scattered around Jerusalem. James and John went to visit Jakob. Andrew and Philip went to buy some supplies. Zacchaeus asked Matthew to come see him. Judas was walking around the temple when two men came up to him.

"Look, I don't believe it," Spero said. "Those demons, Dismal and Murky, are talking to Judas."

"Dismal and Murky are two of the worst demons," I said. "Why would they want to talk to Jesus' disciples?"

"They want to know Jesus' schedule. They want to meet him alone. Judas, it's a trap!" Spero yelled.

"Murky and Dismal are offering to pay for this information. The disciples know that you don't pay to see Jesus. Judas, don't listen to them!"

Judas returned to the other disciples. He asked Andrew and Philip, "A couple of men asked about Jesus' schedule. They wanted me to set up a meeting with him. What do you think I should do?"

"A couple of men approached us about seeing Jesus. I love bringing people to Jesus, but something felt wrong," Andrew answered.

Philip said, "I told them Jesus would be teaching in the temple, but they want to see him alone. Do you think we should warn Jesus about these men, or should we bring them to him?"

Andrew replied, "Jesus tells us not to worry. He can calm storms, walk on water, and heal the sick. Jesus can handle two people."

"Oh, Philip, Andrew, Judas, don't fall for Satan's trap!" I yelled. They couldn't hear me.

I was watching the temple when Judas asked to speak with a member of the ruling council. He entered a side room where the captain of the temple guard greeted him.

"Is it true that you are willing to pay for information about where Jesus is staying?" Judas asked.

"Oh, we know where he is staying. We need to know where he goes to pray at night. Do you have this information?" the captain of the guard asked.

"Tomorrow night, we will celebrate Passover, and Jesus will go to pray after that," Judas replied. "I could slip away and tell you where he's headed."

"Excellent. Here are thirty silver coins. This information is very valuable to the high priest," the captain said. "Meet me here tomorrow night, and we will go visit Jesus. I want to meet him."

"Thank you, sir. I will be here," Judas replied.

"Oh, Judas, don't steal the money. If you don't show up to tomorrow night, I will find you, and you will not like what I will do to you," the captain of the guard growled.

Judas left the temple with a jingling bag of coins.

I felt the jolt of an All Angel Command, and soon the cosmos were filled with angels returning from Earth to heaven. I noticed that Gabriel and the Archangel Michael kept watching Jerusalem. Every time they looked, I also looked. I didn't know what was happening, but I wasn't going to miss it.

Jerusalem, the Upper Room

Tonight was Passover. Where would Jesus celebrate? With Mary and Martha in Bethany, with his family in the olive groves around Jerusalem, or somewhere else? Peter and John walked into Jerusalem and talked to a man carrying a water jug—a most unusual sight. They followed him into a house and upstairs to a large room. Seeing that the tables were ready, Peter and John bought unleavened bread, wine, bitter herbs, and the lamb for the meal. They arranged the food on the table and waited.

"Here come Jesus and the disciples," I pointed out to Spero. Jesus and the disciples entered the house. They washed their hands and sat down for the Passover meal.

"What is Jesus doing?" I asked as Jesus stood up, removed his outer robe, and tied a towel around his waist. After pouring water into a basin, he knelt before the disciples.

"He's washing their feet!" I yelled. "The Lord of the Universe is washing the feet of sinful men. Amazing!"

The lowest slave washed people's feet. An honored guest like Jesus would never do so. Peter tried to stop Jesus from washing his feet until Jesus said, *"If I don't wash your feet, you are not one of my people."* [40]

When Jesus returned to the table, he asked his disciples, *"Do you understand what I did for you? I did this as an example for you. So, you should serve each other just as I served you."* [41]

Jesus spoke to Judas, and he hurried away. I knew what Judas was going to do. I asked to go to him, but I was told, "Judas has made his decision."

Jesus picked up some unleavened bread and thanked God for it. Breaking it into pieces, he said,

"This bread is my body that I am giving for you. Eat this to remember me." 42

The disciples watched Jesus as they passed the pieces of bread around the table. They nibbled at the bread and then ate the whole piece. They kept watching Jesus. We could see wonder on their faces.

Then Jesus picked a cup of wine and thanked God for it. He said, *"This wine is my blood, which will be poured out to forgive the sins of many and begin the new agreement from God to his people."* 43

Jesus handed the cup to John, who took a sip and handed the cup to the next disciple. The whole time the disciples were passing the cup, their faces never lost their look of wonder.

Singing, Jesus led the disciples toward the Mount of Olives. As they walked, Jesus reminded his followers that he would soon die and they would run away. Peter said, "I'm not running away. You can count on me."

"The truth is, tonight you will say you don't know me. You will deny me three times before the rooster crows," Jesus answered. 44

"Not going to happen. Even if I die, I'll be with you," Peter replied, and the others echoed his answer.

Jesus led the disciples to garden. He said to them, *"Sit here while I go there and pray."* [45]

Jesus found a quiet spot and spoke to his father. *"My Father, if it is possible, don't make me drink from this cup. But do what you want, not what I want."* [46]

Several of the angels asked, "What cup is Jesus talking about?"

"The cup of suffering and death. Jesus will become the sacrifice for all mankind," one of the chief angels explained. "Jesus must die for the sins of all people or they could never enter God's presence in heaven."

All the angels started talking to each other: "Jesus is going to die?" "Die for people?" "Why?" "Die for sinners?" "Why?" "I don't understand."

Jesus continued to talk to his father while his disciples slept. Suddenly, there was a rustling of wings as an angel descended to Earth. The angel touched Jesus' head, hands, feet, and back. Then he returned to heaven. I floated toward this angel to ask why he had gone. Then I saw Jesus move. I fell to my knees and didn't move again that night.

Jesus walked toward his disciples and said, *"Stand up! We must go. Here comes the one who will hand me over."* [47]

Jerusalem, Trials

I looked toward Jerusalem and saw Satan disguised as a wealthy merchant talking to the high priest. "Don't worry; you are doing the right thing. This Jesus is dangerous. I've sent two of my best men to see that nothing goes wrong."

I saw a line of torches winding their way up the Mount of Olives toward Jesus. Judas, followed by Murky and Dismal, led the line. A shiver ran down my back. *This is bad,* I thought.

"Judas did meet with the temple guard. How could he do that?" I cried to Spero.

Spero shook his head.

Judas walked up to Jesus, placed his hands on his shoulders, and kissed him on the cheek.

"Grab him!" the head of the temple guard yelled. Several of the temple guards grabbed Jesus' arms and held them behind him. Peter jumped into action and attacked a servant; cutting off his ear.

Jesus said, *"Put your sword back in its place."* [48] Then Jesus touched the servant's ear and healed him.

"I do wish Jesus would call us down. I'm watching for any sign that he wants us to come," I said to Philos.

"Just a flick of his finger, and I would swoop down," Philos responded. "Why doesn't he defend himself?"

"I don't know; I just don't know."

The disciples ran away just as Jesus had said. They quickly blended into the dark of the garden. Several guards started to follow, but Dismal yelled, "We've got the man we want. Let's go!"

Jesus was tied up and taken to the house of the high priest. I was amazed at the lies people told about Jesus, but their stories didn't agree. The high priest paced around the room and yelled, "Get me some decent witnesses! The Romans won't kill Jesus unless we can prove he has broken Roman law."

Spero punched me and said, "Look! Peter is here, and there's another disciple. They came back. They didn't leave Jesus."

Peter knelt down close to a fire to warm his hands. A servant girl approached and stared at him. "You were with Jesus," she said as she motioned toward the high priest's house.

"I don't know what you are talking about," Peter replied.

The angels in heaven groaned when Peter denied knowing Jesus.

I asked if I could go down and talk to Peter. Lt. Parebo said, "Peter was warned."

Peter walked away from the fire, and another servant saw him. Pointing at Peter, he said, "He was with Jesus."

"I don't know the man," Peter growled as he stomped away.

Another man looked at Peter and said, "The way you talk shows that you are from Galilee; you know this man."

Peter glared at the man and shouted, "I swear I don't know him!" As soon as he said these words, a rooster crowed twice. Peter whirled around and saw Jesus looking at him. Peter ran from the courtyard. He sank against the wall of the high priest's house and sobbed.

Spero asked if he could go comfort Peter. "He will be comforted in time," the commander said.

The high priest marched up to Jesus and demanded, "Are you the son of God?"

Jesus answered, *"Yes, I am the Son of God."* [49]

The high priest tore his robe and shouted, "This man insulted God! To the governor's house."

The high priest had gotten Jesus to admit that he was the son of God, and for the Jews this was the worst sin. For Jesus to claim to be related to a god would upset the Romans. The Roman emperor claimed to be a god. The Romans could be persuaded to kill this "make-believe" god. The high priest celebrated; he managed to trap Jesus.

The angels watched. We waited to be sent down. We knew what Jesus had said was true. We watched and waited. We waited and watched, but no order came.

The temple guards beat Jesus. They should have been worshipping him, but they were beating him. When they finished, the guards led Jesus to Pilate, the Roman governor. Pilate did not like the Jews and had killed many of them. Killing another Jew would be easy for Pilate.

The Jewish leaders explained to the governor that Jesus claimed to be king of the Jews and the son of God. Pilate laughed as he looked at Jesus dressed in ordinary clothes with blood running down his face and bruises forming on his back and shoulders. Jesus didn't look like a king or a god to Pilate. Pilate had to judge Jesus, so he asked him, "Are you the king of the Jews?"

Jesus answered, *"Yes, that's right."* [50]

Pilate shook his head as he looked at Jesus. Why did the Jews care that this beaten man claimed to be their king or god? He didn't understand why the Jewish leaders wanted to kill this man. Pilate saw no reason to kill Jesus; he had done nothing against Roman law.

It was early in the morning, and Pilate was tired. Pilate wanted this trial to be over. Then he remembered that during Passover, the governor could release a prisoner. Pilate decided to offer the Jews a choice of which prisoner to release this year. They could choose between Jesus and a violent prisoner. Pilate motioned for silence and announced, "In keeping with tradition, I will release one prisoner during Passover. This year, I will allow you to choose between Jesus and Barabbas."

Barabbas! I remembered Barabbas from many years ago. How many wrong decisions had he made? How much good advice had he ignored? How often had he avoided meeting Jesus? Now he was going to die because the people would choose Jesus over Barabbas, or so I thought.

Satan's demons and workers for the Jewish leaders urged the crowd to yell for Barabbas. I heard the crowd yell, "Barabbas! Barabbas! Barabbas!" A few of Jesus' followers were in the crowd yelling, "Jesus! Jesus! Jesus!" but no one heard them. All the angels were yelling, "Jesus! Jesus! Jesus!" but no one heard us. The people had chosen Barabbas to live and Jesus to die. I was confused.

Pilate was shocked. He'd heard that Jesus healed the sick and fed the hungry. Why would the people choose the violent Barabbas over the miracle worker? His plan had not worked. Pilate had a problem: Jesus. He asked the crowd, "What should I do with Jesus?"

Again, Satan and his demons urged the crowd to yell, "Kill him! Crucify him! Kill him!"

The crowd was out of control. Pilate didn't want a riot. He ordered a bowl of water. Pilate washed his hands and said, "I'm not responsible for this death; you are."

The people yelled back, "We're responsible!"

The soldiers took Jesus away, and Pilate went inside to eat breakfast.

Jerusalem, Calvary

"That's enough beating, guys. We don't want to kill the king of the Jews before we can crucify him. Put the cross on his back and march him to Calvary," the head of the execution squad ordered.

I shuddered as Jesus stumbled through the streets and the crowd jeered at him. Several women pushed their way through the crowd. Mary and Mary Magdalene were trying to reach Jesus. I asked to go comfort these women but was told, "God is with them."

They reached Calvary, a hill outside Jerusalem, and the WHOMP, WHOMP, WHOMP of the hammer driving the nails into Jesus' wrists and ankles echoed through the Universe. Angels gasped and the women cried. Tears ran down my face. *How could they be crucifying the Lord of the Universe?* I wondered. *Fight, Jesus! Fight!* I thought.

Then Jesus said, *"Father, forgive them. They don't know what they are doing."* [51]

Spero stared at his hands. "How long have I had my fists clenched?"

My shoulders sagged as my body relaxed. No fighting today.

I looked around Jerusalem.

Peter paced back and forth whispering, "I said I didn't know him."

Peter, Jesus has forgiven you. I heard him say so.

Pilate wrote something and handed it to a soldier who ran to Calvary. The soldiers at Calvary nailed it to the cross where Jesus hung. All the angels swooped low to read the sign. It said, "This is the King of the Jews."

The high priest and others walked toward Calvary. People yelled, "If you are God, come down!" "You saved others, but you can't save yourself?" "Come down, maybe we'll believe you are the Savior!"

Satan and his demons celebrated in the streets of Jerusalem.

Susanna and Joanna wept at Susanna's home. Yael suggested that they pray. All three knelt together.

Matthew and Zacchaeus read the scriptures together. Zacchaeus invited Matthew to stay in his Jerusalem house, but Matthew decided to stay with the disciples.

Joab watched the crucifixion and sobbed into his prayer shawl.

Uncle Aram went to the temple and fell on his knees crying, "God forgive us. God forgive us." The temple guards grabbed him and threw him out of the temple.

Jairus walked with his daughter near the Pool of Siloam and tried to answer her question about why the High Priest wanted to kill the man who had saved her. He couldn't.

At Jakob's campsite, three brothers sat in silence. Suddenly, John stood up. "I'm going to see Jesus one more time."

"I can't do it," James said.

John left, and James and Jakob remembered the time Jesus had helped them fish.

John walked up to Mary and held her hands. Jesus looked at Mary, his mother, and said, *"Dear woman, here is your son."* [52] Then he looked at John and said, *"Here is your mother."* [53]

Mary whispered to John. He nodded and ran toward the hills surrounding Jerusalem. When he returned, he was holding an ivory box. Mary held it close to her heart.

The sun was high in the sky, but it gave no light. Night covered Jerusalem. Jesus shouted, *"My God, my God, why have you left me alone?"* [54]

All the angels fell to their knees. Sin filled Jerusalem. The earth quaked to avoid it, the smell of decay filled the air, screams of terror ripped through the sky, and the coldness of death stalked the streets and alleys of the city.

Now I understood what was happening. The prophets told of a Savior, a perfect person, who would be killed for sinful people. Jesus was perfect, and they were killing him. Not because he deserved to die, but because people do.

Jesus shouted, *"It is finished."* [55]

All the angels fell face down to worship Jesus.

Jesus shouted, *"Father, I put my life in your hands!"* [56] Then he died.

The sacrifice was finished. The terrible day was done.

I looked around Jerusalem again.

A soldier said, "This man was the son of God."

Joseph of Arimathea, a wealthy man and a follower of Jesus, asked Pilate for permission to bury Jesus. Pilate allowed Joseph to take the body.

Mary gave Joseph the ivory box. When Joseph buried Jesus, he sprinkled the frankincense from the ivory box on Jesus.

Nicodemus, a Jewish leader who had spoken with Jesus, helped bury Jesus.

Mary Magdalene followed Jesus' body to the tomb.

The high priest asked Pilate to place a guard at the tomb so no one could steal the body.

Satan and his demons rejoiced over the death of Jesus.

Peter continued to sob, and his brother Andrew tried to comfort him.

The disciples prepared for a very sad Sabbath.

In heaven, the angels waited for what was next.

Mary, the mother of Jesus, walked with John toward Jerusalem. They were walking through the city when someone ran into them and knocked them down.

"Watch where you're going!" John yelled.

"Sorry, on a mission for the high priest. John, is that you?"

"Zadok, where are you going in such a rush?" John answered.

"You haven't heard what happened at the temple?" Zadok asked.

"I've been busy this afternoon," John answered as he helped Mary stand up.

"A most amazing thing happened. Amram and I were replacing the bread in the holy place because it is the Sabbath. We had put out the new bread and were leaving with the old bread when we heard a ripping sound. The curtain in front of the Most Holy Place tore from the top down. We dropped the bread, fell to our knees, and covered our heads. I thought I would die, but I didn't. We jumped up and ran to the high priest," Zadok said as a crowd gathered around him. "I didn't know the high priest could run so fast. He decided to sew up the curtain. If it weren't so serious, it would be funny. The first needles were too short, then the points too dull, and finally the thread broke. I'm looking for a tentmaker to help with this project."

"There's a tentmaker studying with Gamaliel who lives near the water gate," a voice in the crowd said.

"Thanks, I'll head there," Zadok said. "Talk to you later, John."

Mary and John watched Zadok run down the street. John looked at Mary and said, "What does that mean?"

Mary smiled and said, "I think the high priest has lost his power. God welcomes everyone into his presence, not just the high priest. I'm so tired, John. Please, let's go home."

Soon they were sitting with the other disciples and followers of Jesus.

In and Around Jerusalem

As soon as the soldiers rolled a large rock in front of the tomb, SAAs were sent on missions again. Philos went to Jakob and his family. Spero went to Jesus' brothers and their families. I sat down to watch Earth when the commander came toward me. "The Angelic Council has come to a decision, Felix," he said.

"Yes, sir," I said as I gulped.

"I convinced them that you are very valuable on Earth. You will be sent on missions again, but you will not be placed close to Jesus. You can't control your stars while near him. Only Jesus' followers may shine on Earth."

"Oh, thank you, sir," I said. "I'll stay in control while I'm on Earth."

"Breathe and hum, breathe and hum, Felix," the commander said as he walked away.

I felt a tingle and pulled up a hologram of two women cooking stew. One was Sarah, Joab's wife. Eloooree! Earth, here I come.

I arrived as a twelve-year-old boy beside a campground on the Mount of Olives near Jerusalem. Miriam and Sarah were cooking stew. The rich peppery smell filled the air. I asked if I could have some stew.

"If we give you some, there won't be enough for our families," Miriam stated.

"Remember Jesus told us to feed the hungry. We can share with this boy," Sarah said.

"Sarah, Jesus is dead. Why should we do what he said?" replied Miriam.

"Because he was right. The high priest and the governor were wrong; Jesus was right."

"Sarah, be quiet. You could get us into trouble saying things like that. We don't know who is listening," Miriam answered. "We don't have time to talk. Soon the sun will set and we must stop working. We need water to wash for the Sabbath. Sarah, go get the water, and I'll finish cooking."

"No," Sarah said. "Young man, if you will draw water from the stream, we will give you some stew. Miriam, I'll help you finish cooking. We won't break the law, and we'll get everything done."

I hurried to draw the water before the sun set. At dinner, I sat next to Sarah's husband, Joab. He was the same Joab I had rescued from Ferox.

"You shouldn't have gone, Joab," Sarah said. "It's so sad. I can't believe he's dead."

"Don't be so sad. Jesus said he would return on the third day," I said.

"Boy, Jesus is dead. I saw him die. I saw them bury him. The dream is over; it's finished," Joab answered.

"What about Lazarus? Jesus raised him from the dead," I said. "You must have heard about Lazarus."

"Of course, I have. Jesus raised him. We don't have a Jesus to raise Jesus. Who's going to raise him?"

"God will raise Jesus," I replied.

"Do you really think it's possible?" Sarah asked.

"With God, anything is possible," I stated.

"Then why didn't God save Jesus?" Miriam asked.

"This terrible day had to happen to fulfill the prophecies," I said. "You remember the suffering servant prophecies of Isaiah 53? Psalm 22 told us exactly what was going to happen today, and Psalm 16 reminds us to be faithful. Jesus will rise from the dead. Even Hosea told us to wait for the third day."

"He's right. I don't know the Torah as well as you do, Joab, but I do remember Isaiah 53 and Psalm 22," Sarah said. "Oh, Joab, I can hardly wait until Sunday."

"Please, Sarah, don't get your hopes up," Joab said. "Jesus was dead when they put him in the tomb."

"Oh, Joab, I must hope. I must hope that it's not over, that Jesus will rise from the dead," Sarah said. "It's been a long, hard day. I'm going to sleep, if I can."

I filled the water pots and headed down a path. Eloooree! flip, flip, flip, and back to heaven.

Saturday morning, I was in Jerusalem at the temple. The death of Jesus was the talk of the men at morning prayer. The disciples were hiding. They feared the temple authorities and the Romans. Satan and his demons, still disguised, were parading around Jerusalem, rejoicing in the death of Jesus.

I was speaking to Nicolaus of Antioch and Stephen when Slimatus crept into the conversation. "What are you talking about?" he asked.

"I'm a convert to Judaism, and don't understand much about the Savior," Nicolaus said. "I had hoped that Jesus was the Savior. I don't know what to believe now that..."

"I can tell you this much: Jesus is dead. You can believe that," Slimatus answered.

"No, Jesus said he would rise on the third day," I replied. "That's tomorrow. Hold on to your hope until tomorrow. What Jesus said, he will do."

"I hope you're right, but it seems too much to hope for," Stephen said. "I would love to see Jesus again."

"It is too much to hope for. Jesus is gone. Forget about him," Slimatus said as he walked away.

"Don't forget about Jesus. He's coming back," I said.

After the morning prayers, the men went home for the Sabbath meal. They asked me to join them. I felt the jolt of an All Angel Command.

"I'm sorry, but I must go home. Hope to see you again. Jesus is coming," I said as I dashed outside the city and headed to heaven.

I entered my reports in the database. I had to be on my best behavior. When I finished, I glanced at Jerusalem.

I checked on the disciples. They were huddled together in the upper room. Peter was slumped in the corner, and Andrew was trying to talk to him. John sat next to Mary with his head in his hands. Mary Magdalene fixed a Sabbath meal, but no one ate. The quiet was shattered by the blowing of a ram's horn at the temple. The Sabbath was over.

I checked on Joab; he and his family were fine. Uncle Aram and Amos were walking in the olive groves around Jerusalem. I looked at Joanna and Susanna.

Joanna had picked up her cloak and said to Susanna, "I'm going to see Mary. Would you like to come?"

"I have an appointment with my son, Mahlon. I worry about him. All he thinks about is money. Give my love to Mary. I'll see you tonight."

Joanna walked to the hiding place of the disciples. She knocked on the door. Everyone jumped and stared at the door. Mary Magdalene said, "Who's there?"

"It's Joanna. Let me in."

Mary Magdalene unlocked the door, and Joanna slipped in.

"Did anyone follow you?" Peter asked.

"No, I don't think so," Joanna replied as she stepped toward Mary. The two women hugged and wiped tears from their eyes. Mary, Joanna, and Mary Magdalene sat in the corner and remembered Jesus.

"I need to go to the market," Mary Magdalene said. "I'm going to buy spices and oils so I can properly anoint Jesus' body tomorrow morning. Does anyone want to go with me?"

"I'll go," Joanna said as she patted Mary's shoulder and stood up. "I promised Susanna I'd see her again tonight."

"John, take Joanna to my family's camp and give her the blue bottle I have there," Mary said. "Joanna, when you and the other women go to anoint Jesus' body, please use the myrrh in the blue bottle. It was given to me when he was born; now it can be used for his death."

"I saw it today. I'll get it for Joanna," John replied.

Mary reached into a green velvet bag and gave Mary Magdalene a gold coin. "Use this to buy the spices you'll need. It's the last gold coin I have."

The women and John slipped out the door into the darkening night. First, they went to Mary's camp, and John found the blue bottle. Joanna and Mary Magdalene made plans to meet at sunup the next morning. Joanna returned to Susanna's home in the city. John and Mary Magdalene went to the market where she bought the spices and herbs she needed. They returned to the upper room where everyone was asleep.

Outside Jerusalem

The SAAs were watching the tomb where Jesus was buried. We knew he was going to rise from the dead because he said he would. We just didn't know how. Would chariots of fire take Jesus to heaven as they took Elijah? Would Jesus walk from Earth to heaven as Enoch did? Would the Father call Jesus as Jesus called Lazarus?

I listened to the soldiers guarding the tomb. One soldier, Brutus, said, "I don't like guarding a tomb. I'm not afraid of any man, but the dead—that's different. This criminal was different."

"How do you know?" asked Gaius, another guard.

"I was there when he was whipped. Prisoners will either beg for mercy or yell curses at us, but he did neither. He barely made a sound."

"Strange."

"In fact, the whipping was so boring that we found a robe and draped it over his shoulders. Then Publius made a crown of thorns and stuck it on his head. We pretended to bow before the king of the Jews. Oh, he was a sad-looking king. Still, he didn't react."

"Some people claim that this prisoner was a god. Did he seem like a god to you?"

"I wasn't at his death, but Publius told me that he was human enough. He couldn't even carry his cross to Calvary. They had to get someone to help him. While he was on the cross, he admitted that he was thirsty."

"Doesn't sound like a god to me," Gaius answered.

"They gambled for his robe. It was woven in one piece, and they didn't want to tear it. Publius won it, and he showed it to me. It was ordinary. His sandals were in such bad shape that no one wanted them. Every god I know dresses much better than this guy. The centurion Drusus thought that this fellow might be the son of a god, but I don't agree."

A column of red smoke rose out of Jerusalem, followed by many smaller wisps. Satan and his demons were fleeing Jerusalem. The ground began to rumble; the sky filled with light as an angel descended from heaven. Gaius screamed and collapsed to the ground. Brutus didn't even scream; he just collapsed.

The angel moved the stone away so all could see that the tomb was empty. He waited. The soldiers recovered and ran away.

Shortly after sunrise, Mary Magdalene, Joanna, and several other women came to the tomb, carrying spices to anoint Jesus' body.

"Don't be afraid. Jesus is not here. Go tell his disciples that Jesus has risen from the dead," the angel said.

The women ran to Jerusalem and dashed into the room were the disciples were hiding. "Jesus is gone, and we don't know where he is!" Mary Magdalene cried.

"Is it possible that he has risen?" Joanna asked.

"Could it be true that Jesus is alive?" asked Mary, the mother of Jesus.

"Yes, no, I don't know!" Peter shouted as he ran out the door, followed by John. They charged through the streets of Jerusalem, through the gate of the city, and into the garden. John reached the tomb and looked in; there was no body in the tomb. Peter ran into the tomb and looked around. All he saw were burial clothes. Jesus was gone.

Peter shouted, "Hallelujah, he is risen!" Then he whispered, "Oh, no. He is risen. How can I ever face Jesus after denying him? He must hate me."

No, Peter, Jesus doesn't hate you. He has already forgiven you, I thought.

The disciples were confused. Had the women really seen an angel who said Jesus was alive? Peter and John had returned with the news that the tomb was empty, but they hadn't seen Jesus or an angel. Mary Magdalene came in rejoicing about seeing Jesus in the garden, but he disappeared. She didn't know where he was now.

Thomas paced back and forth across the room. "Please, sit down, Thomas. You're driving me crazy!" Matthew said.

"I can't. I need to know what happened," Thomas answered.

"Thomas, please take me back to my family," Mary said. "I want to check on them."

"I'll take you," John said as he stood up.

"No, John. You need to rest. Thomas needs exercise," Mary answered. "Thomas, I also need you to go to Joseph of Arimathea's house and pick up a white box for me. Let's go. I need exercise, too."

The disciples, fearful of the Romans and the Jewish leaders, locked the door and closed the windows as soon as Thomas and Mary left.

Bang! Bang! Bang! Someone was pounding on the door. The disciples eased the door open. Cleopas and another follower pushed their way in.

"We've seen the risen Lord!" they shouted.

"When? Where? How?" the disciples demanded.

"We were walking to Emmaus when a stranger joined us," Cleopas said. "We told him about the arrest, crucifixion, and the empty tomb."

"This stranger must not have been anywhere near Jerusalem if he didn't know about the death of Jesus," one of the disciples said.

"He explained the scriptures to us beginning with Moses and continuing through all the prophets. I learned more about the Savior in that walk than I ever learned at the temple," Cleopas responded.

"I wish I could have heard this scholar speak," a disciple said.

"We asked him to join us for dinner. He took bread, gave thanks, and broke it. That's when I realized that the stranger was Jesus. He is alive! I walked with him today. I broke bread with him today."

"What happened next?"

"He vanished. Oh, I wish I could see him again."

A presence filled the room; it was Jesus. The door was locked and the windows were closed.

Jesus said, *"Peace be with you."* [57]

Terror struck the disciples. They had run away when Jesus was arrested. Could he ever forgive them? Was this a ghost? Would he haunt them? The disciples trembled as they watched this being.

Jesus held out his hands and said, *"Why are you troubled? Why do you doubt what you see? Look at my hands and my feet. It's really me. Touch me. You can see that I have a living body; a ghost does not have a body like this."* [58]

It was Jesus. Some disciples fell to their knees; some raised their hands in praise. Their Jesus was here; their Jesus was alive!

Jesus asked, *"Do you have any food here?"* [59]

Several disciples hurried to give him some broiled fish. Jesus took it and ate it, just as they did. The women's story was true. Peter and John's story was true. Mary Magdalene's story was true. Cleopas's story was true. Praise God!

Then Jesus disappeared.

Soon Thomas returned. "Why are you so happy?" Thomas asked. "When I left, you were fearful. What has happened?"

"Jesus was here. He is alive!" the disciples shouted.

"I don't believe you. It must have been a dream. I want to see the nail marks on his hands and feet. Until I see that, I don't believe you," Thomas replied.

Cleopas, Mary Magdalene, and the other disciples tried to convince Thomas, but he refused to believe unless he saw Jesus with his own eyes.

In heaven, the angels celebrated and celebrated. The Lord's Army chanted, "Elbildo," the cherubim zipped through heaven making loops and whorls of color, and the seraphim sang, "Glory, Glory, Glory." The SAAs shouted Eloooree! and flipped and leaped in the air. Death is defeated, Satan is shattered, and God rules.

Monday morning, the disciples got up, prayed, and ate. They didn't know what else to do. They told stories about being with Jesus. Peter even acted out walking on the water to Jesus. Everyone but Thomas laughed when Peter pretended to sink. Thomas sat in the corner watching and listening, but not saying anything. Nathaniel suggested they should go to Bethany.

Thomas said, "No, I want to stay here. Jesus might come again."

"I hope he comes again," Nathaniel said, "so you can see him and I can see him again."

"I like your idea, Thomas. I'll stay with you," Peter said.

"I think we all want to stay. We all want to see Jesus again," Andrew said.

The disciples spent the next week waiting for Jesus to come. And then he was there.

He stood in front of Thomas, and Thomas fell to his knees.

Jesus said, *"Put your finger here. Look at my hands. Put your hand here in my side. Stop doubting and believe."* [60]

Thomas looked up at Jesus and said, "My Lord and my God!"

Jesus said, *"You believe because you see me. Great blessings belong to the people who believe without seeing me!"* [61]

Jesus spoke with his disciples, and then he disappeared. Thomas ran to the window and looked for him. Then he ran out the door and ran down the street looking for Jesus. "Where did he go?" Thomas asked when he came back.

"We don't know, and we don't know how to find him," James said.

"Jesus told the women that he would meet us in Galilee," Peter said. "Let's go to Galilee."

Galilee

After all the excitement in heaven, I went to the Majestic Forest to rest when I felt a tingle. The hologram showed a woman selling plums along the road between Jerusalem and Jericho. Eloooree! to Earth I go.

I took on the form of a young girl when I landed. I looked at my woman; she was sick. No one would buy plums from her. She spotted me. "Please, buy some plums. They're good, I promise," she begged. "My family needs the money."

"You look tired. Go rest under the tree, and I'll sell your plums," I said.

She was afraid I would steal from her, but she finally decided to rest. "I'll rest, but I'll be keeping my eye on you," she said as she stretched out under a tree. Soon she was sound asleep.

"Fresh, juicy plums! Get sweet plums for your journey!" I called out all day. Most of the plums were gone when down the road came seven men, including Peter, Thomas, Nathanael, James, and John.

"Fresh, juicy plums!" I shouted.

"They look good," Peter said.

"They are good. Where are you headed?" I asked.

"To Galilee," James said.

"To see Jesus," John said.

"The Jesus who rose from the dead?" I asked. "Tell me about him."

The disciples sat down, ate plums, and told stories about Jesus. What a fabulous mission this was.

"We need to get going," Peter said. "Here's the money for the plums, and thank you for listening to our stories about Jesus. It's good to tell someone about him."

They headed down the road. I woke the woman up and gave her the empty baskets and a handful of money.

"Oh, my," she said. "So much money. Here, you take some."

"No, thanks. I enjoyed myself," I said. I walked over the hill. Eloooree! flip, flip, flip, zip.

I enjoyed writing this report. When I finished, I went to the Reflection Grotto to think about all the stories the disciples had told me. I knew some of the stories, such as the feeding of the 5,000 and raising Lazarus from the dead, because I had been there. Other stories were new to me, such walking on the water, quieting a storm, or finding money in a fish's mouth. I looked toward Earth to thank them. They were discussing the future.

"What are we to do when we get to Galilee? I was studying to be a teacher, but now I don't know what to teach," Nathanael said.

"You can teach what Jesus taught," James answered. "At least you can still teach. Fishing will never satisfy me. I don't know what I'm going to do."

"Jesus will come to us in Galilee and tell us what to do," Thomas said. "I have no doubt about that."

"Yes, we know you never doubt, Thomas," Peter replied.

"At least I didn't deny him," Thomas retorted.

"You just ran away!" Peter yelled.

"Stop it!" John said. "Jesus would be so disappointed in us fighting like this. Pick up the pace. I want to get to the Sea of Galilee and see Jesus again."

"Me, too"

"Me, too."

"Me, too."

"Me, too."

"Me, too."

"Me, too."

"Me, too," I thought.

When they reached the Sea of Galilee, they set up camp and waited, but Jesus didn't come.

"Do you think we are in the right place?" Nathaniel asked. "Maybe we should go to Capernaum."

"Peter, what did you think we should do?" James asked.

"The only thing I know to how do is fish," Peter replied. "Into the boat anyone who wants to go." Seven disciples piled into one fishing boat and fished all night.

"Look, there is someone on the beach."

The stranger on the beach called out, *"Friends, have you caught any fish?"* [62]

"No."

"Nothing."

"Not a bite."

Jesus shouted, *"Throw your net into the water on the right side of your boat. You will find some fish there."* [63]

The disciples looked at each other, shrugged their shoulders, and threw the net into the water. They caught so many fish that they could not pull the net into the boat. John tilted his head and stared at the beach. He remembered another miraculous catch. "It's Jesus!" he yelled.

Peter jumped into the water and swam toward shore. The other disciples rowed to the beach. Jesus had set up a fire to grill fish for breakfast. He said, *"Bring some of the fish that you caught."* [64]

Peter was the first to obey. He pulled in the net full of big fish and helped grill them on the fire. Jesus served his disciples bread and fish. Several times, Peter started to say something to Jesus, but he stopped and hung his head.

Jesus motioned for Peter to follow him. As they walked down the beach, Jesus talked to Peter. When they returned to the others, Peter was smiling. He whispered to Thomas, "Jesus forgave me for denying him. He forgave me three times, once for each time I denied him. I love Jesus. He is so good."

"He forgave me for doubting him," Thomas said. "He is good."

While in Galilee, Jesus continued to teach his disciples. One day he said, *"All authority in heaven and on earth is given to me. So go and make followers of all people in the world. Baptize them in the name of the Father and the Son and the Holy Spirit. Teach them to obey everything that I have told you to do. You can be sure that I will be with you always. I will continue with you until the end of time."* [65]

Jesus told his disciples to go to Jerusalem and wait for the Holy Spirit.

Road to Jerusalem

I joined other SAAs to watch Earth. We heard Thomas' voice and looked toward Galilee.

"Peter, do you know who or what the Holy Spirit is?" Thomas asked.

"I think the Holy Spirit will teach us, but how or when, I don't know," Peter replied. "What do you think, James?"

"The Holy Spirit will guide us, but the only instruction we have now is to go to Jerusalem. We need to go there," James answered.

The disciples started the long walk from Galilee to Jerusalem.

They had been on the road for several days when I felt a tingle and saw a hologram of seven hungry men. I dove into the cosmos and landed in the sheep pasture, just barely missing a sheep. I was a young boy, about ten years old. The sun was low in the sky, so I made dinner. I opened my pack and found beans, a knife, and a pot. I made a bean stew with onions and greens.

Seven men came walking over the hill. Peter called to me, "Boy, do you have any food you could share?"

"Yes, sir, I do. You are welcome to some of my stew," I replied.

"Thank you very much. We have walked all day, and we are tired and hungry," Peter said.

"Rest here on the soft grass. There is a cool stream just over the hill," I replied.

I fed them bowl after bowl of stew. It never occurred to them that I served more stew than my pot would hold. It wasn't the feeding of the 5,000, but it was the feeding of the seven very hungry disciples.

As they ate, they told stories about Jesus. I knew some, such the raising of Jairus' daughter and the healing of a crippled man who was lowered through the roof. I heard new stories about the healing of a Roman soldier's servant without even seeing him and the raising of a widow's son from the dead. I loved hearing more stories about Jesus.

They said their evening prayers, lay down wrapped in their robes, and slept. In the morning, they filled their water skins in the nearby stream and continued toward Jerusalem.

I returned to heaven with a triple somersault and a shout of Eloooree! After writing up my report on feeding the seven very hungry disciples, I watched them.

I felt the jolt of an All Angel Command. We were to meet at the Golden Boulevard. I took a quick peek at Earth before heading to the meeting place. There was Peter leading the followers of Jesus up a hill near Bethany. As they reached the top of the hill, Jesus appeared and said, *"The Holy Spirit will come on you and give you power. You will be my witnesses. You will tell people everywhere about me— in Jerusalem, in the rest of Judea, in Samaria, and in every part of the world."* [66]

Jesus rose up until he disappeared in the clouds. Everyone stared at the clouds. I heard a rustle of wings and saw a flash swoop down from heaven.

Two angels in radiant white robes appeared beside the believers.

"Why are you looking up in the sky?" one angel asked.

"Jesus has gone to heaven, but he will return the same way," the other angel said. Then the angels disappeared.

"When is he coming back?" a believer called out. No answer.

"What are we to do?" another believer asked.

"Wait for the Holy Spirit," one of the disciples answered. "Let's go back to Jerusalem."

Sounds of singing filled the air as the disciples led the people back to Jerusalem.

Heaven

I started singing along with them. It was wonderful until a blast from the golden trumpets filled the air. The golden trumpets—the signal that Jesus was coming home. My curiosity was going to get me in big trouble this time. I had to get to the Golden Boulevard, and fast.

The music of the gold trumpets continued to echo. The music traveled around the universe, bouncing from planets to stars to meteors, telling all that Jesus was home. I dashed toward the music.

The angelic choir began to sing: "All praise and honor and glory and power forever and ever to the one who sits on the throne and to the Lamb!"

Their song rang throughout the universe. Everyone was doing his best for Jesus, and that gave me time. I dashed behind the angelic choir. They were focused on Jesus and didn't notice me. Where were the SAAs? I had to find them.

The Lord's Army was the next to welcome Jesus home. I tiptoed past it. The army would not appreciate my being late.

As Jesus passed, the seraphim stilled their six wings and bowed to the Lord. Their fiery light brightened in the presence of his love. The cherubim also stilled their wings and bowed their faces to the ground as Jesus walked by. As I crept behind the cherubim, I saw the SAAs lining the Golden Boulevard.

I made a dash for the SAAs and slid in next to Philos. As I arrived, he dropped to his knees. I knelt as I caught my breath. We bowed our heads as Jesus walked by. When I saw the scars on his feet, I remembered that terrible day when he was killed and the glorious day when he arose. He loves the people of Earth so much. "Eloooree," I whispered.

Forty steps after Jesus, the Archangel Michael walked, followed by Gabriel. Next came the trumpeters, the angelic chorus, the Lord's army, the seraphim, the cherubim, and then the SAAs.

Philos and Spero walked side by side as they fell
into line. Gaudo and I were following them, but
the commander grabbed my arm. Gaudo walked on
ahead. The commander pulled me back. "What were
you thinking? You ignored an All Angel Command,"
he said. "This is the most important day in heaven,
and you were watching Earth. Walk beside me
so you don't wander off again." The commander
tightened his grip on me. I was really in trouble this
time.

We were the last SAAs to get in line. The people
in heaven were waiting for us to pass. Adam and
Eve followed us. Then came Abraham and Moses;
Noah and Jonah; John the Baptist and his mother
Elizabeth; Joseph the prince of Egypt and Joseph
the husband of Mary; Isaiah and Ezekiel; Ruth and
Sarah. On and on the people came.

All in heaven formed a semi-circle in front of the
throne. The people were in the front rows. I saw
David and Esther offer their crowns to Jesus.

Jesus walked to his throne and sat at the right
hand of the Father. A wall of fire appeared behind
the Father and the Son. It was the Holy Spirit. A
strong wind enveloped the throne and radiated
through the universe. Then came the light—a light
so bright, so pure, so holy that nothing could look

at it. The angels and the people bowed low to the ground to worship God. Slowly the light dimmed; the seraphim began to sing, "Holy, holy, holy." The angels and the people sang back:

ELOOOREE, GLORY TO GOD, ELOOOREE, GLORY TO GOD, FOREVER, AMEN!

Scripture References

1. "Don't be afraid. I have some very good news for you—news that will make everyone happy. Today your Savior was born in David's town. He is the Messiah, the Lord. This is how you will know him: You will find a baby wrapped in pieces of cloth and lying in a feeding box" (Luke 2:10–12).

2. "Praise God in heaven, and on earth let there be peace to the people who please him" (Luke 2:14).

3. "If you work hard, you will have plenty. If you do nothing but talk, you will not have enough" (Proverbs 14:23).

4. "Why did you have to look for me? You should have known that I must be where my Father's work is" (Luke 2:49).

5. "Let it be this way for now. We should do whatever God says is right" (Matthew 3:15).

6. "This is my Son, the one I love. I am very pleased with him" (Matthew 3:17).

7. "A person does not live only by eating bread" (Deuteronomy 8:3b).

8. "You must not test the Lord your God" (Deuteronomy 6:16).

9. "Get away from me, Satan!" (Matthew 4:10a).

10. "Respect the Lord your God and serve only him" (Deuteronomy 6:13).

11. "Dear woman, why are you telling me this? It is not yet time for me to begin my work" (John 2:4).

12. "Fill the water pots with water" (John 2:7).

13. "Now dip out some water and take it to the man in charge of the feast" (John 2:8).

14. "Take the boat into the deep water. If all of you will put your nets into the water, you will catch some fish" (Luke 5:4).

15. "Don't be afraid. From now on your work will be to bring in people, not fish!" (Luke 5:10).

16. "Friend, your sins are forgiven" (Luke 5:20).

17. "Why do you have these questions in your minds? The Son of Man has power on earth to forgive sins. But how can I prove this to you? Maybe you are thinking it was easy for me to say 'Your sins are forgiven.' There's no proof that it really happened. But what if I say to the man, 'Stand up and walk'? Then you will be able to see that I really have this power" (Luke 5:22–24).

18. "I tell you, stand up! Take your mat and go home!" (Luke 5:24b).

19. "Who touched me?" (Luke 8:45).

20. "Someone touched me. I felt power go out from me" (Luke 8:46).

21. "My daughter, you are made well because you believed. Go in peace" (Luke 8:48).

22. "Don't be afraid! Just believe and your daughter will be well" (Luke 8:50).

23. "Don't cry. She is not dead. She is only sleeping" (Luke 8:52).

24. "Little girl, stand up!" (Luke 8:54).

25. "This is my Son, the one I love. I am very pleased with him. Obey him!" (Matthew 17:5b).

26. "Stand up. Don't be afraid" (Matthew 17:7).

27. "A man was going down the road from Jerusalem to Jericho. Some robbers surrounded him, tore off his clothes, and beat him. Then they left him lying there on the ground almost dead" (Luke 10:30).

28. "Which one of these three men do you think was really a neighbor to the man who was hurt by the robbers?" (Luke10:36).

29. "Martha, Martha, you are getting worried and upset about too many things. Only one thing is important. Mary has made the right choice, and it will never be taken away from her" (Luke 10:41–42)

30. "There was a man who had two sons. The younger son said to his father, 'Give me now the part of your property that I am supposed to receive someday.' So, the father divided his wealth between his two sons" (Luke 15:11–12).

31. "I am the resurrection. I am life. Everyone who believes in me will have life, even if they die. And everyone who lives and believes in me will never really die. Martha, do you believe this?" (John 11:25–26).

32. "Move the stone away" (John 11:39).

33. "Lazarus, come out!" (John 11:43).

34. "Take off the cloth and let him go" (John 11:44b).

35. "Bring that man to me!" (Mark 10:49).

36. "What do you want me to do for you?" (Mark 10:51).

37. "You can see now. You are healed because you believed" (Mark 10:52).

38. "Zacchaeus, hurry! Come down! I must stay at your house today" (Luke 19:5).

39. "Today is the day for this family to be saved from sin. Yes, even this tax collector is one of God's chosen people. The Son of Man came to find lost people and save them" (Luke 19:9).

40. "If I don't wash your feet, you are not one of my people" (John 13:8b).

41. "Do you understand what I did for you? I did this as an example for you. So, you should serve each other just as I served you" (John 13:12b, 15).

42. "This bread is my body that I am giving for you. Eat this to remember me" (Luke 22:19b).

43. "This wine is my blood, which will be poured out to forgive the sins of many and begin the new agreement from God to his people" (Matthew 26:28).

44. "The truth is, tonight you will say you don't know me. You will deny me three times before the rooster crows" (Matthew 26:34).

45. "Sit here while I go there and pray" (Matthew 26:36b).

46. "My Father, if it is possible, don't make me drink from this cup. But do what you want, not what I want" (Matthew 26:39).

47. "Stand up! We must go. Here comes the one who will hand me over" (Matthew 26:46).

48. "Put your sword back in its place" (Matthew 26:52).

49. "Yes, I am the Son of God" (Mark 14:62a).

50. "Yes, that's right" (Matthew 27:11b).

51. "Father, forgive them. They don't know what they are doing" (Luke 23:34).

52. "Dear woman, here is your son" (John 19:26b).

53. "Here is your mother" (John 19:27a).

Scripture References

54. "My God, my God, why have you left me alone?" (Mark 15:34b).

55. "It is finished" (John 19:30).

56. "Father, I put my life in your hands!" (Luke 23:46).

57. "Peace be with you" (Luke 24:36b).

58. "Why are you troubled? Why do you doubt what you see? Look at my hands and my feet. It's really me. Touch me. You can see that I have a living body; a ghost does not have a body like this" (Luke 24:38–39).

59. "Do you have any food here?" (Luke 24:41b).

60. "Put your finger here. Look at my hands. Put your hand here in my side. Stop doubting and believe" (John 20:27).

61. "You believe because you see me. Great blessings belong to the people who believe without seeing me!" (John 20:29).

62. "Friends, have you caught any fish?" (John 21:5b).

63. "Throw your net into the water on the right side of your boat. You will find some fish there" (John 21:6a).

64. "Bring some of the fish that you caught" (John 21:10).

65. "All authority in heaven and on earth is given to me. So go and make followers of all people in the world. Baptize them in the name of the Father and the Son and the Holy Spirit. Teach them to obey everything that I have told you to do. You can be sure that I will be with you always. I will continue with you until the end of time" (Matthew 28:18–20).

66. "The Holy Spirit will come on you and give you power. You will be my witnesses. You will tell people everywhere about me—in Jerusalem, in the rest of Judea, in Samaria, and in every part of the world" (Acts 1:8).

CPSIA information can be obtained
at www.ICGtesting.com
Printed in the USA
LVHW041028011020
667641LV00002B/85